About the Author

The author was a distinguished professor in the civil engineering department at the Indian Institute of Technology in Delhi. Despite his background in technology, he had a strong appreciation for literature. Following his formal retirement, he began writing stories and poetry in his native language and in English. His writings mainly reflected Eastern philosophy and fantasies.

Assorted Stories

Tushar Datta

Assorted Stories

Olympia Publishers
London

www.olympiapublishers.com
OLYMPIA PAPERBACK EDITION

A CIP catalogue record for this title is
available from the British Library.

ISBN: 978-1-80439-759-6

This is a work of fiction.
Names, characters, places and incidents originate from the writer's
imagination. Any resemblance to actual persons, living or dead, is
purely coincidental.

First Published in 2024

Olympia Publishers
Tallis House
2 Tallis Street
London
EC4Y 0AB

Printed in Great Britain

Dedication

I dedicate this book to my dad.

Fifty-Fifty

I sat down with a cup of coffee after returning to my apartment from the office. There was a note on the table, "Gone out to eat. Back by eight." It was from my partner. The digital clock on the table flipped from eight to ten. I was getting bored and thought to have a shower. There were varieties of shampoo, shower gel, soap, shaving cream, and toothpaste in the bathroom. They made quite an inventory. After the shower, I changed into a loose dress. Gone was the grime of one bizarre day; I felt fresh.

She returned at ten o'clock with a shopping bag in her hand. I guessed the contents of the bag could be anything from A to Z; two-thirds of them were already in the apartment. She pulled out a pack of ice-cold beer. So I cracked open a can of beer.

For a year, she was my business partner. She received half of my daily earnings, as well as my car, apartment, and household. As I used the metro, her share of the car's gasoline consumption was nearly one hundred percent.

"It's about the cruise tomorrow," she said.

"You mean the cruise on Dover Lake?" I asked, pulling some sausages from the fridge. Then I cut some onions and tomatoes and browned them in a frying pan to make something tasty. She took two, while I took three.

After she finished them, she said, "Exactly, but we'll take the cruise from the mall side."

"That's fine; it's more expensive but worthwhile," I replied. "Do you think you'll be able to make it by six?" she stated.

"I'll be out of the office by five."

"That is the wise thing to do. Guess the bill you have to pay for two people," She retorted.

"A thousand."

"Make that twelve hundred," she said.

"I think you're right. A two-hundred-dollar margin is good enough," I replied.

Throughout the conversation she was cleaning her ears. She took out a new cotton swab and fingered it for a while. "What about booking? Aren't we late?" she asked.

"Not a single company operates; moreover, it's a weekday. No doubt, tourists would be there from all over the place, but it's only two tickets. We can buy on the spot," I answered.

"Wonder if tourists ever enjoyed the cruise. They enjoy their own company with drinks and dance. The place could be the desert as well," she said.

"You mean a desert cruise?" I asked.

"Well, something like that; sand in place of water!"

"We had it on the jeep in Arizona."

She cleared away the beer cans and glasses and put the kettle on.

"How about a cup of coffee?"

"Good idea," I said.

Then, while waiting for the water to boil, she listened to rock music. When the kettle whistled, she made the coffee, singing along with the rock. I spent the entire time reading the evening newspaper. It was a charming domestic scene anyone would enjoy. Except for the cruise, which is in suspense, I might have been delighted.

She smoked a cigarette and stretched out on the sofa by the window after finishing her coffee. A refreshing breeze blew in through the window. I went over to sit beside her and got an ashtray. The cat suddenly appeared from nowhere and jumped up on the sofa – his chin resting on her feet. It was a cute cat with silky fur on the body, the tip of the tail straight, and eyes so small and innocent that it couldn't tell the difference between a tennis ball and an orange. She stroked his head.

"Best thing in your apartment to share," she said. "We had one when I was young. Mom fed him a variety of things. In the morning, he used to get milk and canned cat food; in the evening, a handful of dried fish or fatty meat. He used to eat all of them. His litter box was cleaned daily as he did not like it dirty. He often had diarrhea, and if it did not go away after two days, he was given some medicine. He would have his ears cleaned at two day intervals with olive oil and a cotton swab. He often fought it out, and Mom took care so that he did not claw the furniture. She would trim her claws once a week and bathe him every so often. After the bath, she would dry him off with a towel and give him a good brushing."

"Did your mother do anything else?" I inquired.

"I'm not sure at the moment."

"Your mom took good care of him," I complimented.

She returned to the subject of cruises, saying, "Most tourists take the early ones." They're done by eleven p.m. or so. We could avoid the early ones and have a better chance of getting tickets."

"Don't worry about the tickets," I replied, "the only thing to worry about," she snatched my words, "is tomorrow's plans, which are always in suspense."

"I might come back from the mall after ten, and you might as well take a refreshing shower by then," she jokingly suggested.

After a while on the sofa, she said, "Let's go to bed." Before I could prepare myself, she dropped onto the bed, murmuring some numbers, and fell asleep.

Time does not move; events move. Events make a year; the time stands frozen. A year finally ends.

She had finished her breakfast with beckons and eggs and was getting ready to leave with her small suitcase the next morning. "You owe me some money," she said abruptly.

I looked at her, studied her face for a moment, and then took out a checkbook slowly.

"Could you repeat the number you murmured last night?"

She repeated it.

That's what I wrote on the check. It was exactly half of a year's hidden savings!

She took hold of the suitcase.

"May I drop you?" I asked.

"A year has passed; I had a free breakfast."

"You might as well have a free ride," I replied.

She got into the car and pulled out a cotton swab. While cleaning her ears, she described how she used to play with her brother as a child. I was wondering how she knew about my secret savings the entire time she was talking. I was tempted to ask her, but I resisted. She asked me to stop the car near the mall, got off, and said, "You have my number; give me a call if you need me."

I tried one last time to ask her how she could know my secret savings, but she had vanished into the crowd.

I turned my car toward the apartment. "What difference would it make now?" I said to myself. A year has gone by. Events will bring the end of another year.

COVID-19

In the early morning hours, there was a long queue of vans on one side of a narrow road. Each van carried a lifeless body covered by a white sheet. The air was deafeningly quiet. The van's drivers were resting on their seats, a few dozing, and quite a few smoking away the time. In front of the queue was a gate. The billboard above the entrance relayed, "COVID-19 Morgue." To deal with an unexpected rise in deaths due to Covid, the municipal authority established a special morgue.

The silence of the surroundings was tersely broken by a hue and cry. Two individuals were seen running parallel to the queue while carrying a dead body on their shoulders. The police officers, who had been watching the line from a distance, rushed toward the individuals. By the time they arrived, they had loaded the body onto the carrier of the third van, from where a young man suddenly emerged from the white cover. He jumped out of the truck, dashed across the road, and vanished into the sparse tall grasses on the field that stretched from one side of the road. The officers were bewildered. Before deciding what to do, the two persons who carried the dead body also fled.

One officer decided to chase the young man, while the other began searching the two people. The second officer eventually tracked down the two people who were hiding behind a broken shed. As he approached, they took a few hundred rupees bills out of their pockets and struck a deal with the officer to appear near the queue when it would begin moving. The other officer's story was different. He had to play a long game of hide and seek in the field before he could win. Both the officer and young man made their way to the morgue after the young man surrendered. The two started talking while they were on their way.

"What is your name?" the officer inquired.

The man quickly presented a death certificate to the officer. He stared at the person for a moment before saying, "The name on the certificate reads Amit Sur." "Are you the one?" The man gave a nod.

"Do you believe you're dead?"

"Based on the certificate, I'd have to say yes."

"That means I'm speaking to a ghost."

"In some ways, it is."

"Is there another way to look at it?"

"That's up to you to figure out."

"What evidence do you have that you are Mr. Amit Sur?" The man drew his identity card from his wallet right away. The officer looked at the photograph on the card and then back at him before returning the card.

We need to go to the hospital that issued the death certificate; verify your home address and your father's name," the officer explained. They walked in silence for quite some time. The officer then broke the silence, "Why did you jump out of the van and flee? What exactly were you doing there?"

"My task was over as the two individuals brought the dead body to the van," the man replied and continued, "until then, I had to lie on the van's carrier like a dead body. That's the deal that was struck behind the scenes. For two reasons, I jumped out of the truck and ran away. First and foremost, I was alive and capable of performing those acts. Second, I was holding a place in the queue of dead bodies – no one accompanying the dead bodies would have tolerated it."

"So, you admit your guilt?" the officer asked, looking at him.

The man promptly answered, "Yes."

"While we would be preparing the charge sheet against you, you might get some credit for this candid admission," the officer said.

The man retorted, "Sir, I told you the truth. However, as the investigation progresses, you will discover that I had been declared dead by the hospital. They had issued a death certificate, which I had shown to you. As a result, I was legally dead as long as I was covered by the white sheet. How a dead body could jump out of a van is a mystery that medical science must solve. I can't think of anything on which you could implicate me unless you have a record of my candid admission to you."

"No, I did not record your frank admission. As a result, you don't have to be concerned on that front. However, just so you know, the charge sheets are primarily based on motives. The motive appears to be clear. However, framing it in the guise of law is difficult," said the officer.

After walking in silence for a while, they arrived at the morgue. The officer discovered the other officer relaxing with an earthen pot of tea under a tree's shed. Leaving the young man on the road, he made a move toward the tree. Upon reaching there, he began conversing with the officer. A tea vendor approached him and offered him a similar pot of tea.

The morgue's gate was about to open. The drivers of the first few vans in the row were preparing to enter the gate. The two people who had been hiding behind the shed were gradually emerging from their hiding places. After the tea break, the officer who had apprehended the young man returned to him. He was standing alone so far, in a remote corner of the road, out of sight

15

of the drivers.

Soon after the officer reached the man, a police jeep arrived. Along with the man, the officer got into the jeep. The officer took the front seat while the man sat in the back of the jeep. The driver was told to drive to the hospital. There was a snarl of traffic on the main road as if there had been a mishap. The jeep was unable to move steadily. Now and then, it had to come to a halt. The officer had a feeling it would take some time to get to the hospital. So he struck up a conversation with the man.

"How did you end up in the hospital?" the officer inquired.

"Sir, I should be frank with you and answer every question of yours truthfully because you didn't record my frank admission last time," the man replied. He then continued, "Speaking frankly does not always imply speaking truthfully. Many people, to be honest, tell lies. I'm not going to dare to do that to you. To answer your question, I was admitted to the hospital emergency department as a Covid patient. Two people drove me to the emergency unit. They struck a deal with me that I would have to leave the emergency room as a dead person in five hours and travel to the morgue in the hospital's van. They offered me twenty-five thousand bucks for it. It was handsome money for me."

"Had they managed the doctors to end your life in five hours, or did you offer to die on your own in that time?" the officer inquired.

"Nothing of that sort. The two persons were well aware of my qualifications. Many people like me are doing this type of business in the market. They picked me up for their work," the man responded.

"Interesting!" the officer said as he turned his head toward him and continued, "The police are unaware of this group and its operations. Please provide me with your credentials."

The man began, "Sir, this is not a mafia group in the traditional sense. We are a dedicated group that provides a variety of services to the public. Only through those services do we earn a living. The main service that we offer is holding spots in various queues for people who cannot wait in line for an extended period. Another useful service that we provide is a proxy. We also provide a variety of other unimportant services. As for the credentials, most of us can speak and write in at least two to three languages. We can run in a zigzag pattern faster than ordinary people, suddenly vanish, and perform various types of acting, including mod dances. Only a few members of this group are capable of playing the role of a deceased person. And I happen to be one of them."

"Great that you have proficiency in two to three languages and have some magical skills. What puzzled me was how you played the role of a deceased person. Is it a parody or a reality?" the officer inquired.

The man replied, "Sir, you would think that I am talking a load of nonsense, but as I said before, I dare not be dishonest with you. We learned the art of dying for a short period from a great yogi who hails from the Himalayas. It took me about two years to master it. It is a yogic practice that most yogis residing in the upper parts of the Himalayas perform to survive inclement weather. From a scientific standpoint, it is a type of hibernation that is found in the animal kingdom. It might be of a little higher order than simple hibernation. In this case, the heartbeat comes to a halt."

"I've heard this type of story since I was a child, but I never believed it," the officer explained. Now that you've said you can do it, I may have to reconsider my belief, after a thorough investigation, of course.

"Did you have Covid and pass away in the hospital?" The jeep entered the hospital's portal before the man could respond.

They both descended from the jeep and entered the hospital. The officer entered the chief administrator's office. The man was following him. The administrator motioned for them to take their seats and inquired the officer as to the reason for his visit. The officer took the man's death certificate, held it up to the officer, and asked, "Is this certificate issued by your hospital?"

The administrator examined the certificate and replied, "Yes."

"Did you double-check all of the information in the certificate?"

"We reproduce the same information that is provided at the time of registration."

"Do you verify the identity of the individual who registers the patient?"

"We take the person's signature and mobile number as a formality. We do not validate them as such. However, as a precaution, we collect advance payment and the income tax card number. Furthermore, we only give the dead body to the person who registers the patient."

"That's a fairly cautious approach," the officer retorted and continued, "Take a look at this man." He motioned with his finger to the man."

The administrator looked him over and said, "He appears to be perfectly all right. Do you want him admitted to the hospital for some unexplained symptoms?"

The officer replied, "He was admitted to your hospital and declared dead. The death certificate on the table in front of us is his death certificate."

The administrator said, "There must be some confusion. A dead person cannot sit in front of me or beside you. Let me check what's wrong?" He dialed the numbers of the people who needed to be reached at his office. Three people appeared in a short period and formed a circle around the table. The administrator explained the situation to them. They began comparing information on the death certificate to those scripted on the computer and discovered no errors in any of the information on the certificate.

One of them then questioned the man, "If you were dead, how did you get the death certificate? It is only provided to the individual who admitted you to the hospital. The death certificate is not folded and stuffed into the pocket of a dead man."

The man took out his identity card and handed it over to the administrator calmly. He looked at the photo on the card, raised his head, and looked at him. Then, he flipped the card over to double-check the information. For a while, silence prevailed.

The administrator finally said, "Well, the information provided in the card corresponds to those registered at the hospital. There is only a possibility that there could be a second man with an identical name and having the same father's name. The address could have been printed incorrectly on the card. This type of blunder is fairly common. However, there the major question remains: How did the death certificate get to you?"

The officer cut in, "We might ask him about how he got the certificate later. Before that, it is necessary to confirm that he is the man who died in this hospital. I believe your emergency room is being videotaped. You could easily trace the episode of his death, and we could all verify if he was admitted on the date specified in the certificate and died in this hospital."

"That's a good idea," the administrator said. The three

19

people exited the room and returned a short time later with video clips. In no time, the video was on television. The man's intent while watching TV was utterly different from that of others. Others were curious about the story, while he was interested to see his actions on the screen. As he watched different video parts on the screen, he suddenly realized he was a fantastic actor. His performance was so natural that he congratulated himself. A dream, a dream that he could do better in Bollywood only surfaced in his mind.

The first video clip began with his arrival at the emergency room. Doctors in Covid uniform rushed to him, monitored his temperature and blood pressure, took blood samples, and swapped pieces. The first clip came to an end there. In the second clip, he was placed on a bed with an oxygen mask over his head. A tube supplying fluid was attached to his arm. A few injections penetrated the plastic bottle, filling the liquid. He was finally hooked up to a cardiac monitor. The third clip was brief and insignificant; doctors and nurses passed by him, watching his cardiac monitor and fluid bottle. He was lying on the bed like a perfect patient, coughing now and then, which drew the nurses' attention. The third clip went on until he became breathless. In the last clip, the oxygen mask was placed over his mouth. The oximeter indicated adequate oxygen concentration, but the cardiac monitor displayed a weak signal. Doctors rushed to him; they continued the cardiac massage, but the signal dwindled and dwindled until it became flat at one point. During the final scene, he did an excellent job of mimicking the movements of a dying person. Everyone who saw the video was confident that he was the man who died in the hospital. "It is indeed a surprise, if not a mystery, how the same man who died in front of us in the video is sitting before us," the administrator said after the video show ended. It defies all medical explanations.

One of the viewers asked him the same question that he asked before, "If you were dead, how did you get the death certificate?"

Except for the officer, everyone looked at him with interest. "When I woke up, I found the death certificate on my lap," the man replied calmly. Hearing his response, the hospital personnel, including the administrator, were stunned for a brief moment.

After a while, they looked at each other——puzzled. Finally, the administrator dialed the Covid specialist to get to the bottom of the mystery.

The Covid specialist walked into the room, took a seat, looked around, and asked, "What's the matter?" You all appear to be very disturbed and perplexed."

"Yes, we are," the administrator replied before briefly recounting the incident to the Covid specialist. The specialist was staring intently at the man the entire time the administrator was narrating.

"It appears I saw the man in the emergency unit," the specialist said after he finished.

"It is difficult to remember anyone in particular because ten to fifteen people die every day due to Covid. The doctors in the emergency room are still working nonstop to manage the situation. In any case, could you please turn on the video again?" He went through all of the clips and then remained silent for a while before asking one of the hospital personnel to look for the man's Covid test report. It took some time to track down his test report. Everyone was waiting for the test results with bated breath. The specialist astounded everyone. He stated that the man had tested negative for Covid.

The administrator exclaimed, "Then he had some other

serious ailment that caused his death. The Covid report had not arrived by the time the patient died. If the report had been available, the course of treatment would have been different, and the patient might have survived. However, this is not the hospital's fault. His obvious symptoms were those of Covid, and some of the blood test results received before his death did not indicate any serious illness." Suddenly, the administrator realized he was speaking something which he would not have uttered. So, he came to a halt and apologized to everyone, admitting that he was no doctor and that he made those statements out of complete confusion.

"Even though it appears to be a mystery," the Covid specialist retorted, "two or three similar cases have already been reported. The hospitals declared them dead, but on the way to the morgue, they were resurrected. They felt as if they were awoken from a deep slumber. Experts believe that Covid plays tricks in a variety of situations. Its symptoms are highly ambiguous in their manifestation. It is now thought that the double plus variant of the Covid has begun to spread. The variant's symptoms are completely unpredictable. They can range from no symptoms to symptoms resembling death. Because the demand for beds is so high in each hospital, it is difficult for hospital administrators to keep the dead bodies for an extended period. As a result, this type of case is on the horizon. This young man, I am certain, was a victim of the Covid's double plus variant."

Everyone appeared to be satisfied with the episode's explanation. However, the main question remained unanswered: "How did the death certificate reach the man while he was dead?"

The administrator stared at the officer and asked him how he tracked down the man. The officer simply stated that he found him alive in a van near the morgue. The specialist was pleased with the response because it confirmed his theory. However, none of the information could explain how the man obtained the death certificate.

Then, a slew of questions was directed at the man. He deflected them all like an arrow aimed at a person. The questions ranged from "Are you married?" to "Do you have children?", "Do you have a will for your property?" They changed their view when hospital officials discovered he was single and barely making ends meet on his meager earnings. They took his death certificate as useless other than loading the dead body onto a van en route to the morgue. The administrator stated that whoever received his dead body wished the certificate to be burned along with his body.

There was a collective sigh of relief among the hospital staff. They congratulated the man on his new lease on life. In particular, the specialist patted him on the back to survive the Covid's double plus variant. The officer took leave of the administrator and walked out of the room. The man trailed him. The jeep was waiting for them near the gate. "I don't have to verify your father's name and address any longer, but the investigation isn't over. So hop in the jeep and follow me to the police station," the officer told the man as he climbed into the jeep. The man got into the jeep and occupied the back seat. As they arrived at the police station, the officer exited the jeep and went to his chamber.

He was followed by the man. "Your performance in the video was excellent," he said as he asked the man to take a seat and ordered two cups of tea. Then, he continued, "So, how was your interview with hospital personnel? There are circumstances when unreality contrives to create an impression that overwhelms reality. That's exactly what happened. But there are a few things

I need to know from you."

The man replied, "As I said before, I shall be honest in providing you with any information you need."

Meanwhile, the tea had arrived. The officer took a sip of the tea and began, "I have a few confusions in the entire story. I'd like to clear them up and get an accurate picture of the situation. Only on that basis, I will frame the charge against you. There is no doubt about the theme: you were hired to hold a spot in the queue for the dead body. You offered your services because it was your business. However, the following questions arise: How did the two people who admitted you to the hospital estimate a five-hour time frame for your death? Given that twenty-five thousand rupees is a sizable sum, how did those individuals agree to pay you the sum? How did you stimulate your body's temperature? How did the doctors perceive you as a Covid patient? How much money did the two people spend to keep you in the hospital as a Covid patient? Is it worth spending so much money just to get to the front of a long queue? Finally, am I to believe you can defraud medical science?"

After finishing his cup of tea, the man turned to the officer and said, "Sir, you asked me a lot of questions. Instead of answering them one by one, let me tell you everything I know. This might answer all of your questions. If it didn't, I would provide any additional information you would require."

He began, "The two people who contacted me came from a wealthy family. Their father had been admitted to the hospital fifteen days before I was admitted. He tested positive for Covid. Despite the best treatment available, his condition worsened over time. He was already on the ventilator when the two people called me. Three-quarters of his lungs were dormant. His chances of survival were almost non-existent. According to the doctors, his life could end within twelve hours since I was admitted to the hospital. The two people called me around nine p.m. and told me they would admit me to the hospital between eleven and twelve a.m. Knowing the death rates due to Covid in various hospitals, they made some estimations. If their father died by the afternoon the next day, they would have to wait in a long queue to enter the morgue. It was highly likely that the waiting period might be one to one and a half days in the current state of affairs. With that estimate in mind, they gave me only five hours to die so that I could be at the front of the queue in the early hours of the morning. Their estimate was accompanied by some financial calculations as well.

"All hospitals are now robbing money in the same way that malls do during the festive season. A Covid patient in a single bedroom is charged a lakh rupees per day in all major hospitals. They had already spent nearly twenty lakhs of rupees on their father's treatment. So they didn't mind paying an extra fifty thousand rupees to get to the front of the morgue queue. That's also why they only gave me five hours to die so they wouldn't have to pay the hospital more than fifty thousand rupees for my treatment.

"As soon as the two persons contacted me in the night, I took a high dose of a garlic and ginger combination. This combination has been known to raise the body temperature above 100 degrees and keep it there for five to six hours. I also started doing a neck exercise that warmed up the jaw and ear. I was able to successfully raise my body temperature immediately before being admitted. There was some uncertainty in the procedure used to increase the body temperature, but it worked positively. The uncertainty brought in some amount of tension, which in turn raised both my blood pressure and body temperature. To induce a dry cough was no big deal. Because of the current situation, anyone admitted to the hospital's emergency department with a fever and a dry cough was treated as a Covid patient. So, when I was admitted to the hospital, I was immediately labeled as a Covid patient."

The officer was paying close attention to what the man was saying. "Your story had a good number of interesting points, and it answered all of my questions except one," he said after the man finished. He continued, "That insightful question is about the dying art you learned from the Himalayan yogi. Despite having seen its demonstration in the video, I still take it with a grain of salt."

The man stared at the officer for a moment before responding, "So you want, I might give you a live demonstration here itself. You will only need to give me fifteen minutes of your time for this. I'm going to lie down on the floor for fifteen minutes, relax, and take away my breath. You could then check my breathing and pulse rate."

"No, I would never ask you to do that. I believe what you say because there are so many unknowns in heaven and on earth that are beyond our comprehension," the officer said.

Suddenly, the man became extremely polite and retorted, "Sir, I had admitted my guilt to you from the beginning. You assured me by saying that you would give me some credit for my frank admission during the framing of the charge against me. I am willing to share half of my income with you so you can relax a little more in framing the charge against me."

For a while, silence hung between the two. The officer then broke the silence, saying, "If it had been a different case, I would have considered your offer. But, after reviewing the entire episode of the case, I decided not to charge you for two reasons:

first, I promised you that I would give you some credit for your candid admission, and second, and most importantly, you have provided a great service to a dead man by allowing him to reach heaven in the final leg of his journey without having to endure grueling waiting in a long queue. Service to a man, dead or alive, is a good human act. It is now time for you to depart."

Flute

Among the many pilgrim places, 'Har ki Pauri' has a special appeal to Indian pilgrims. Wrapped up in a host of mythological stories, it carries a rich spiritual heritage of ancient India. Spiritual seekers from all over the country gather in this place: some of them perform holy rituals, while others purify their souls by taking a holy dip in the Ganges. The traveling monks of various sects add a spiritual aroma to the place.

'Har ki Pauri' stretches over the narrow strip of land that divides the torrential flow of the Ganges into several streams running through the city of Hardwar. The brown muddy water flowing through the streams is colder than ice. To take a dip in that water is unimaginable without having a deep reverence for the Ganges. The Ganges here is not just a river but is the mother Ganges, the goddess whom the pilgrims worship for the liberation of their souls. The 'Ganga Arti' performed in the early hours of the morning and evening in praise of the goddess is a spectacular sight enjoyed by pilgrims and tourists alike. 'Har ki Pauri' has a special appeal among the elderly. It's the allure of having limitless freedom, which they crave every time they let go of the burdens of their worldly responsibilities. It's similar to the joy of playing flute in the vast valley of music.

Goutam had the desire to take his father and his favorite professor to the 'Har ki Pauri', which was only a few kilometers away from Roorkee, ever since he joined the building research institute there. The professor was not only his guide but also a family friend who supported them during difficult times. Goutam was looking forward to meeting his father and professor in Roorkee. Finally, it happened.

"So, how is everything? Seems like an awful long time since I saw you last," said the professor.

"Indeed, it's after long years that we are meeting," said Goutam's father, "you look almost the same."

"But you look much younger," replied the professor, "I heard people losing age, but for the first time, I saw it myself."

"All is the grace of the Almighty!"

Goutam's father was in his sixties, with black curly hair, toned muscles, healthy teeth, and bright eyes. When the professor looked at him, a memory from his past flashed through his mind.

Goutam's father was a patient in a hospital. A slew of plastic tubes hung from his body. The professor gave him a sidelong glance. His face was pale, his cheeks bare of flesh, his eyes sunk, and his hair was untidy. He was staring at the ceiling, possibly watching nothing. As the professor approached, he uttered something in a choking voice that the professor could not hear. He looked at him curiously. Goutam's father waved his hands as if he was bidding farewell to everyone. Professor bent down upon him and whispered, "Like flowers scattered in a storm, man's life is a long farewell, as they say, but don't worry, you will be fine soon——so the doctors say." With a dismayed smile on his face, he retorted, "Can you listen to the distant sound of the flute? Perhaps not. It's ringing in my ears. It is music that liberates one from all shackles and transports one to eternal joy. I don't lament my departure, but I am disappointed that I was unable to complete my duties and must delegate them to my son."

"All souls yearn for freedom," the professor said softly, "but it is only at the end of life's journey that it is attained; but you have a long way to go."

Professor wondered if the man in front of him was the same as the one he had seen in the hospital.

"It appears that time is a great magician," the professor said as they both entered the house.

A delectable lunch was waiting for them. It took them a long time to finish it because the conversation veered off into a variety of topics during lunch. They took a brief siesta after lunch and then set out for Hardwar.

The car pulled out with them. Goutam occupied the front seat next to the driver. It followed the national highway stretching between Roorkee and Hardwar. The tightly packed city streets of Roorkee gave way to sparser housing, then fields and vacant land. On either side of the road stood rows of old stocky trees that towered over the road, blocking out the sun and covering everything in gloomy shadows. Through the trees peeped the gray tiled roofs of small houses, which caught the early autumn sun.

The driver began steadying the wheel to negotiate the twists and curves of the road. By the time the road became relatively straight, the car plunged into a small stretch of forest. The breeze flowing into the car through the half-closed windows turned suddenly colder. At the point at which the forest ended, the broad green farmland spread out in all directions. Small settlements bordered the farmlands. The scenery repeated several times. The car would enter a small forest, come out to a settlement, and then go back into the forest. After about forty-five minutes of driving like this, the car reached a vast area with a wide-open view. Mountain peaks appeared some distance away as they moved as if a hidden mountain range took an impulsive turn to race parallel with the road. The area between the road and the mountain peaks gradually transformed into a valley, with pebbles and boulders strewn about. A few streams separated by sand and boulders appeared after a few minutes. The streams diverged from a river's main course; the road rushed to hug the river bank and continued its journey alongside it. It was the bank of the river Ganges.

The road now became straight, and in view was a cable bridge some distance away. Goutam said to the professor, "That's the famous Ganga Bridge. The river divides there into two main streams, the left one reaching the site of the "Ganga Aarti" on the riverbank, famed as "Har ki Pauri."

They reached "Har ki Pauri" when the sun was setting behind the mountains. The wide stone-paved bank of the river had tarnished into a gray platform. The muddy water flowing down the river with torrential current carried the gloomy shadows of the small temples standing in a row on the other side of the bank. The last rays of the sun fell on the top of the temples, forming cascaded shadows of each one on the other. There's a continuous flow of people pouring into the bank from the landing stairway of the bridge that runs across the river. Few persons were leaning over the railings of the bridge to catch a glimpse of the panorama of the clock tower standing amidst the crowd and the course of the river meandering to the bank.

The priests started preparing for the "Ganga Aarti" lighting the fashioned large oil lamps; the cold breeze that blew along the course of the river was flaring the lighted lamps. The last group of people hurriedly finished their holy dips in the Ganges before the Arti began. A chorus of overlapping sound and music originating from the crowd was spreading in all directions. Suddenly, the clock over the tower struck seven. Moments thereafter, the priests stood in one row contouring the bank of the river. They lowered the lamps to the edges of the water and then raised them as high as their arms could carry them. The radiant flames of the lamp were flickering in space in a lofty attempt to touch the sky. The "Ganga Aarti" began.

The "Ganga Aarti", a devotional ritual that uses fire as an offering to the Ganges, is a tradition that runs over time immemorial. And not just the fire, small vessels made out of leaves with candles and flowers set inside are floated down the river by the pilgrims as offerings to the Ganges. "Har ki Pauri" Ganga Aarti has the deepest appeal to the pilgrims. People, priests, idols, clanging bells, blowing of conch shells, waving of incense sticks, chanting of hymns, and circling the large flaming lamps make it quite a spiritual circus. In the same breath, all of them are synchronized to a single rhythm, which is a splendor that casts a spell on the viewers.

The crowd started thinning out as the Arti was over. In a little while, the bank looked deserted. Except for the tea hawkers and a few vendors selling the toys, who were on their way back, it had only a human occupation of a regular few who slept on the bank of the Ganges. They were lying on the bank gazing at the sky. The professor and Goutam's father made their way to the famous market of Hardwar. They could hear the trailing sounds of the flowing water of the Ganges as they began walking.

There were different types of markets: markets in malls, markets in open plazas, markets along the sides of wide streets, and open markets. The Hardwar market was unique, with shops on either side of a narrow pedestrian road. It was a passage for all: humans to animals and rickshaws to small cars. The whole was a maze of randomly arranged shops selling all types of items. The narrow passage of the road was vibrant with a cocktail of sounds.

Goutam's father stood in front of a shop and picked up a flute. He held the flute over his lips and blew an enchanting sharp melody that, piercing through the bizarre sounds of the market, disappeared in the expanse of the air. The professor looked at him with awe and said to Goutam, "I didn't know he was so expert in playing the flute."

Goutam replied, "Not only in the flute but also his expertise in a variety of musical instruments was known to all. He was a music teacher in a school, and at the same time, he was the music master of a drama group. He had a vibrant musical life."

"For a long time, he had to be out of the music world to settle his family," he continued.

"He wanted to return to the world of music now that he had completed all of his obligations. He wished for a flute from Hardwar."

On their way back to the car, Goutam's father was holding a flute in his hand as if a maestro was carrying his musical instrument. The car pulled off through the highway. On either side of the road, every single noticeable entity appearing, on and off, in their onward journey had disappeared; darkness as one blanket had covered them all. Inside the car, the silence separated the three. Occasionally, a sudden wave of whizzing sound bruised the window glasses of the car as a speeding car passed by. In about forty minutes of drive, they reached Roorkee.

As Goutam's father was about to enter the guest house, he hugged the professor and told him, "It was some enjoyable moments that I spent with you after a long time. Thank you for your company. I'll see you at breakfast tomorrow."

"The same here, see you then," the professor replied.

The following morning, the professor woke at seven a.m. and opened the window. A rush of fresh air entered the room carrying with it a fine melody of the flute that filled the air inside. The professor stood by the window, wholly immersed in it. A sudden knock on the door broke his spell. He stepped toward the door and opened it. In came Goutam with a newspaper in his hand. The professor told Goutam, "I was absorbed in the music; indeed, your father was a maestro."

Goutam said, "In the morning, he woke at five a.m., and since then, he was with the flute; it's not the flute he was playing; he was galloping through an ephemeral world of boundless freedom."

The PhD Professor

He knew everything there was to know about the Ph.D. He was dubbed "The Ph.D. professor." He had long hair, white as snow. They were thin enough to expose the skin up close, but they gave the impression of a scholar from a distance. His brows betrayed his hair, which was black and short. He stood five feet seven inches tall, an average height, and a self-possessed figure with sturdy bones. His nose protruded from his face but stopped halfway before becoming a challenging angle.

The professor excelled in scholastics from early on, a child wonder known to everyone in his locality. And not just schooling, he graduated at the top of his class in the university and went for research to finally become "The Ph.D. professor."

Long years of working with research students helped him develop the hypothesis that students do not require research guides. Instead, they need ghosts who would enter their bodies, lock their brains, and solve their problems. Though performing such an act requires a magical fit that is difficult for a human to achieve, the Ph.D. professor took this as a challenge and made it his life's mission. The world, in his opinion, is mediocrely dotted with a few geniuses who helped the world evolve to its present state.

He was surrounded by the supposedly stupid students who had been abandoned by great professors. Before they got to him, they were in an ocean of uncertainty and desperate to find something to cling to. They found him a lifeboat. The students stayed with him at his home, which resembled a library. Books, articles, and notes were heaving like packs in a warehouse in each room. The whole place smelled indistinctly of old papers; the walls were designed with patches of white sheets used as writing boards. Students managed their stay within small spaces dug inside the heaps of books. There was no better option for them either. But they were happy to discover that they at least existed and were sure of reaching their goals.

On thirteen May 1993, Rajesh arrived at the professor's residence. Like others, he was whirling on and on in the ocean of uncertainty. He was desperately looking for a firm ground on which he could land and maintain his balance, but nothing was in sight. He yearned for anything to cling to, but not even a thread was available. He was, as though, set into a spin of senseless motion, challenging to break. Finally, the unlucky thirteen turned out to be lucky for him.

On the first day, his friends helped him to make a space for himself and comforted him to have a good sleep that night. The next day, he had his first meeting with the professor.

"The Ph.D. professor" sat behind his desk and motioned his finger for Rajesh to sit down. He made his way over, straddling books as if crossing a minefield, and sat down.

"Well, now," said the professor, "you were thrown out of those big ships of knowledge for no fault of yours."

"Not really; I was not up to the mark to stay there," said Rajesh.

"*Hmm*," the professor said, "you seem to be different!"

"My wife also says so."

"Oh, you have a wife!"

"Two kids as well."

"That's all right, but tell me what you are best at?" asked the professor.

"Play with my two kids," said Rajesh.

"What's about the research?"

"I am not good at mathematics, so avoid it. I can play with the computer for hours; perhaps I am good at data handling," Rajesh answered.

"That's fantastic. All of us are good at that. Our brains are supercomputers churning out millions of data every minute," said the professor.

Rajesh looked very happy. He said to the professor, "I am also good at doing odd jobs that students avoid, such as climbing up the hill, fixing an instrument on a mast, and running with a speedometer."

"That's a great talent; very few people have it," the professor replied.

Encouraged beyond his expectations, Rajesh made a gesture to say something more. "Go ahead," said the professor.

"Sir, my genre believes that a student should serve his teacher while learning. This service is unlike any other service. It is a type of service performed in a church or temple to please God and receive His blessings. That blessing is more valuable than knowledge. Only learning reduces one to a collection of meaningless words, jargon, and names. Without the blessing of the teacher, they don't turn into real knowledge. That faith runs in my blood. If you would give me a chance to serve you, I shall be at my best." He continued, "I am sure you would think that all I am saying is a load of nonsense. And perhaps it is so. But just consider, that's all I have got to say."

The professor looked at him for a while and said, "Thanks for being so open. What you said is an example of Eastern learning philosophy. It is quite appealing, though not very obvious. A portion of it is shrouded in mystery and not well understood. In any case, we will have intense interactions. Perhaps I have to enter your body a few times, which is no less mysterious. But service to others is a good philosophy in itself. Tell me in what way you can serve me."

The prompt was the reply, "Anything other than academics."

Rajesh was delighted way beyond his expectations after the first meeting; there was someone who could at least understand him. The immediate consequence was that he surrendered himself to the professor with complete confidence. Admittedly, the course of events brought Rajesh closer to the Professor than others. He became the professor's assistant, and the professor became his family friend.

The professor had a unique way of dealing with the students. Upon entering the student's body, the first thing he did was to remove the feeling of uncertainty from the student's mind as he knew "uncertainty slays a mediocre." At the same time, he recognized that the absence of uncertainty takes away the challenge of research. So, his second move was to implant a cybernetic uncertainty in the student's mind. That gave him and others an impression that his study was full of challenges without truly unsettling him. It was the master craft of "The Ph.D. professor" in the profession, which none of his colleagues possessed. His students used to graduate at the proper intervals of time with a decent image of his work. After graduation, they had to leave the professor's research hub, though.

Like others, the time for Rajesh to leave the research hub had come one day. Accepting it was difficult for him. He went to the professor and told him, "Sir, if you wish to say anything, you may please do so after I finish, but lend me your ears for a few moments. I came here to pursue my Ph.D. It is now finished. I know I don't have any right to stay here anymore, but rights hardly go under the contract; they are won. I have served you throughout these years with complete dedication, as I have done in the service offered in the church. I am sure it did not pass your notice. With that rigor in my service, I feel I have earned the right to stay here for a longer period to serve you again. I believe my words don't mean much to you, and perhaps they are so, but I truly meant what I said."

The professor looked at him straight on his face and replied, "I never asked you to leave my place. What you thought was the convention everyone followed, and it was hard for you to follow that. As for the service, more service means more rights you earn according to your philosophy, and you will never be able to leave this place. I will not ask you to do it, but simply close your eyes and recall the day you arrived here." When he closed his eyes, he saw someone whirling in the same ocean of uncertainty that he was. He realized he needed to make room for that person. He looked at the professor, picked up his luggage, drew a circle around the area he was in, and wrote "Vacant" inside it.

Grandfather's Clock

Rommy awoke at six o'clock in the morning, washed his face, sat alone in the corridor, and gazed out the window. The canal's water level had dropped since the previous day, and it was now running clear. Morning breezes traced random waves through the tall grasses on the opposite bank. An army truck drove toward the hills on a road that ran parallel to the canal. A flock of skylarks flew in a full circle above the canal, landing on the wire fences. Then, one by one, they flew away and were swallowed up by the cloudless sky.

The land rover arrived at ten o'clock, as promised. It was a tourist company's old Land Rover. Rommy and his wife climbed into the back seat of the Land Rover after finishing their breakfast. "You know, there is something wrong up the mountain," said the driver, "I tried to contact my friend up there but couldn't get through. It seems the telephone line is down somewhere. Maybe there's been heavy snow."

"But since yesterday, there hasn't been any snow," said Rommy.

The driver turned his head at an angle and said, "Then, we should go up and check it ourselves."

Rommy nodded.

"When does it start to snow?"

"Wouldn't be surprised if it snowed next week," said the driver. "It will be late November or early December before it starts piling up. Have any experience of winter in these parts?"

"No," Rommy said.

"Well, once it starts piling up, it continues nonstop. By then, there's nothing you can do but rest inside."

"Isn't that boring?" Rommy's wife inquired.

"Well, they don't apply their minds to what's going on, and it wouldn't help if they did. They just spend the winter inside, eating, sleeping, and staying warm."

The road in the hills began to become steeper and curved like a snake. The rustic scenery gradually gave way to a complete facade of dark forest on both sides of the road. Occasionally, there would be a tear in the facade, allowing a glimpse of the flat green fields below.

With one hand on the steering wheel, the driver moved his head around to crack his neck and then looked straight forward to negotiate every curve. A silence followed. Rommy's wife seemed to be in deep thought, and Rommy closed his eyes.

Thirty years since his grandmother passed away, he had been to this place. He cherished a desire to see his grandfather's clock all these years——his grandma narrated to him. So long, he could not make it; now that he set out for it, memories started crowding his mind.

Grandpa had a farmhouse on the other side of the hill. By its side was a vast pasture surrounded by posts where he raised sheep. Grandma said she liked sheep and helped him to raise them. They remembered her face so well that they would flock around her as she entered the pasture. Stories in pieces, grandma narrated, were scripted in mind, and they were afloat.

He could imagine the grandfather's clock——just above the fireplace in the living room in the farmhouse——striking twelve times at midnight. Grandpa used to wind the clock with a big key at that hour of the night, so said the grandma.

The jeep abruptly bounced, agitating everyone, including the petrol stored in a plastic tank. Rommy blinked his eyes open and gazed at his wife. She, too, emerged from her deep thought. The driver was adjusting his grip on the steering wheel. For a few kilometers, the road continued in this manner. The driver abruptly exclaimed, "Look to the left." As Rommy turned left, he noticed a broken mud wall in the dark forest——the mud crumbling away. The view was spectacular as a vast valley appeared through the opening. Ahead of the road, a narrow mountain peak gradually moved in. The mountain's peak had been neatly shaved. The strong wind that blew up the right slope from the valley blew sand against the jeep's windows, turning the mountain's peak into a painting on a light grey canvas.

The weather took a turn for the worse all of a sudden. The light grey sky darkened, giving the mountains and surroundings a gloomy appearance. The winds began to whirl around, wheezing and moaning all by themselves. The driver leaned forward to listen intently, gradually slowing the jeep until he stepped on the brake. He got out of the land rover and turned off the engine. "It rained a lot harder than I thought," he said, tapping the ground with the sole of his shoe.

"The core within is damp, and it fools everyone. Things are different in these parts." He continued, "Ahead of us are dangerous curves with slopes so porous, they would crumble at the slightest shiver. I wish I could take you down to your destination, but better not to take a chance."

"It's okay for walking. You have to walk down another three kilometers from here," said the driver.

"That's all right. Thanks for everything," said Rommy.

The driver said, "The caretaker's son is my friend. I sent him a message. There is a mailbox by the front door. You will find the key to the house in it. If nobody is there, use that." He got into the Land Rover, waved his hand, and was gone.

Rommy and his wife were abandoned. "Let's get moving," Rommy said. The sky was dotted with patches of moist and grey clouds. Below, dense black clouds blew by almost within a hand's reach. The sound of their footsteps on the road reverberated along steep slopes as they walked only three hundred meters. Spring-fed rivulets snaked across their path now and then. They went down and down through many curves until they reached a clear stream. A sturdy wooden bridge spanned the stream. They dropped their packs on the ground, walked up to the stream, and drank some water. They then sat on its side, looking up. The dark clouds passed directly overhead.

Rommy's wife placed her head on his shoulder, closed his eyes, and said, "Let's rest for a while." Rommy, too, had his eyes closed.

Grandma said the grandpa handed over the house to a caretaker who liked the sheep very much. For thirty years, Rommy had no clue as to what was happening there. He heard the caretaker was no more. His son had taken over the job of looking after the farmhouse. Not sure if he stayed there at all. It might be deserted, might be visited by him occasionally, but for sure, the farmhouse existed. The farmhouse that occupied his imagination was a picture painted by his grandmother with stories. It was a two-story wooden house with three bedrooms on the top floor, a large hall, a kitchen, and a guest room on the ground floor. The grandfather's clock hung on the wall beside the fireplace in the large hall.

Rommy told his wife, "Let us move." They climbed the wooden bridge, crossed the stream, and went inside the dense forest. The top of the trees made way for the dark clouds; a few patches of them glided down to make the passages foggy. They walked through the forest for about fifteen minutes.

Suddenly, in front of them appeared the vast, clear grassy land; at some distance away was the big pasture surrounded by wooden poles. Straight on across the pasture stood an old-styled two-story wood-frame house, the grandpa's farmhouse.

The smell of rain was suddenly all over the place. The pasture was enormous. It would take them a long time to get to the house, no matter how fast they moved. Rain could fall at any time. They kept moving, and by the time they arrived at the house, the rain had begun to fall.

The door of the house was closed. Rommy knocked on the door several times. There was no answer. He approached the mailbox. The key was precisely in the same position, the driver said. The key fitted the keyhole remarkably well, and the door clicked open.

"Hello? Anybody in the house?" Rommy shouted.

A silent house, deserted, if not hunted.

Rommy got into the big hall; sofas, chairs, and wall hangings were dusty and scattered. Indeed, the caretaker would not be visiting the house regularly. On one side of the hall was the fireplace, and just by its side, the majestic grandfather's clock was hanging on the wall.

It was almost dark inside. Rommy's wife searched for the light switch. Rommy went close to the grandfather's clock. Suddenly, the hall lit up as Rommy's wife pressed a button. Rommy looked up; a wooden plank hung itself at the corner of the roof in bravura. It might fall anytime, but it didn't fall so far!

The grandfather's clock was big. The roman letters on the clock appeared as if they were under a lens. Below the clock, a brass piece protruded from the wall; on it was an iron box. A winding key was kept on top of it. He touched the key; it was tightly fixed to the chest. With any amount of force, it was not possible to detach it. There must be some magnet inside the box!

"Let's check upstairs," said Rommy. Both went up. There were three bedrooms. Two of them had the same look as that of the downstairs hall. Only the farther small bedroom showed signs of human occupation. The bed was neatly made, and the pillow had a slight indentation. Next to the window were an old table and a chair. There were a few papers and a pen in the drawer. Except for the caretaker's son visiting occasionally, there seemed to be no other person staying there.

They got down to the big hall. Rommy's wife vanished into the kitchen, saying, "See if I can make something for us to eat." Rommy occupied a sofa and looked at the grandfather's clock. *Someone must be there to wind the clock*, he thought; the *needles of the clock flip meticulously to produce the click sound every second.*

Who could be the person? Caretaker's son? He did not appear to visit here regularly. Then, someone else should be staying here. But, the house looked deserted. Grandpa himself? Then, the house must be a haunted one, but that's a wild imagination!

Rommy's wife came with something to eat. They finished them together. Rommy's wife occupied the other sofa. Tired of the long journey, both felt heavy. It only took a few seconds before they fell asleep.

Rommy woke up at the third bell of the clock; after nine more bells, the needles came to a halt. Rommy got up, went near the clock, and touched it's key. Surprisingly, the key was no longer tightly fixed to the box; it was loose. He picked up the key and kept winding the clock until the key refused to rotate. The clock started clicking. As he was about to put the key back in the box, a sudden force dislodged the key from his hand and fixed it back on its lid. He stood frozen and gazed absently at the clock. The time passed by. He didn't know how long he had stood there like that, and when he returned to the sofa, stretched himself, and fell asleep. Only the grandfather's clock had an account of it.

Rommy's wife stroked Rommy to wake up in the morning. She sat by his side and said, "I had a good sleep in the night. Sure, you had a nice sleep too."

Rommy nodded.

All of a sudden, she started laughing. Rommy looked at her. "You have the look of your grandpa." She pointed to a giant painting hanging on the wall just above the fireplace. She continued, "With a mustache, you would look the same when you would grow old." Rommy looked at the painting. His grandpa was smiling at him. The grandfather's clock had vanished from the wall, and in its place was hanging the portrait of his grandpa.

Rommy's wife went to the kitchen to fetch coffee and returned with two cups in her hand. They sat face to face on the sofa as they drank the coffee. Drops of rain tapped intermittently on the window. The time passed slowly. Rommy looked out the window to the vast pasture outside. His mind was full of absurd thoughts beyond any reasoning. He thought he would ask his wife if the painting was hanging there on the wall last night. But he refrained from it. He thought what difference it would make even if she said "yes". After all, he had seen the grandfather's clock and set it in motion right at midnight, like his grandpa used to do.

The Boss

Born the fourth son of a poor mechanic's family in a remote place in Bihar, he left home at sixteen to make a fortune in Dubai. But he found no footing there. He returned home and joined the extreme leftist group known infamously as Naxalites. He was known as an enraged young man and a deadly fighter. He most likely just finished high school. Nonetheless, he had risen to the top of the leftist group by acquiring charisma, oratory skills, and command over the party's cadres. Above all, he honed his ability to exploit the weaknesses of the masses.

He was appointed as the group's boss. His presence was felt because he was manipulating everything from behind. He was a shadowy figure who never appeared in public after assuming power. He established a powerful underground organization and introduced various elements such as politics, finance, bureaucracy, idealism, and communication. Everything was built by him. The government saw it as the group's weakest link. They reasoned that if the boss died, there would be no one to take his place. The group would disintegrate.

The boss put a stop to such an idea. He convinced his party cadres and others that the boss was an invisible entity residing in the 'will' that formed the group's forefront. The ideology was the backbone that held the front together. If the obvious boss died, the entire 'Will' would be passed on to someone else. As a matter of practice, he would then go underground. The boss, dead or alive, was not visible in either case, just as the 'will' was not visible. Though the transfer of the 'will' from one to the other was somewhat mysterious, the people were persuaded by the group's legacy that such a possibility existed. Thus, the government's hypothesis that "the group would fall apart" was reduced to a mere rumor.

The boss was a mediocre leftist cadre before ascending to power. The group used his rage and lethal fighting ability to inflict heavy losses on government forces in battles. Rumor had it that he could fight in space, five feet above the ground, and take on three enemies at once, much like the hero in a class one fighting film. Despite his deadly fighting abilities, he was apprehended and imprisoned on suspicion of plotting the assassination of a key government figure. His incarceration lasted three years. And this turned out to be a watershed moment in his life Official records noted several strange incidents occurred with him during this period. According to the records, he had acute gastroenteritis, which had deprived him of sleep for nearly the entire duration of his incarceration. He had a stomach tumor, according to his medical records. It was large enough to destroy the entire digestive system. The entire stomach would stop working if it exploded. An operation, on the other hand, was out of the question. It could explode at the slightest provocation. When the doctor who discovered it saw the ultrasound film, he was astounded. Having such a large stomach tumor while remaining as active as the average prisoner defied all medical explanations. He was moved from the prison medical unit to an army hospital for special tests.

The tests continued for quite some time without a conclusive diagnosis. They only added to the mystery of how the person was still alive and showed no signs of disability. Furthermore, with acute gastric syndrome and insomnia, it was a mystery how he maintained his singular vitality. Army medical records also revealed a specific symptom the boss experienced at regular intervals—severe abdominal pain that lasted for two days. He needed narcotics to relieve his pain, but they gave him hallucinations. Nobody knew what caused these hallucinations. The army intelligence service was intrigued by these hallucinatory experiences and documented them several times. In about ninety percent of his hallucination sessions, the boss would draw a figure. It looked like a human, but it had a skull for a head. The sketch sparked speculation and prompted the intelligence unit to conduct an investigation.

The intelligence unit's top-secret tests piqued the interest of party cadres. They couldn't figure out why the army intelligence was investigating a stomach tumor in one man. They sparked speculation about a wide range of possibilities. Couldn't they have conducted more sensitive interrogations under the guise of medical tests as a first option? For example, securing spying routes to border areas, escape routes in the event of encounters, and the provisional locations of cadre camps and training centers, which change regularly. The boss was released without being charged after a battery of tests. A deal could have been stalled behind the scenes. Exchange of information in exchange for liberty! But will he be able to pull it off? Even if he did, the information he gave was suspect. The army intelligence, on the other hand, was no fool! The second possibility was that the whole story of insomnia had been twisted. To force criminals to confess, the intelligence unit would deprive them of sleep. Because he was involved in a plot to assassinate a key figure in the government, the boss was subjected to such harsh interrogation. It was anyone's guess whether or not their efforts were fruitful. The boss was a tough nut to crack.

The third possibility was brainwashing. By sending one predetermined wave frequency into the brain, a brainwashing group blocks certain brain activities while opening up new ones. Such tests could have been conducted on the boss. Again, the outcome was anyone's guess. The short of it was that the only people who knew the truth were a few army intelligence officers and the boss himself. So far, the boss had remained silent on the subject.

Another strange fact that perplexed the cadres was that the boss was practically a changed man after being released from prison, as if he had been born again. He miraculously acquired the ability to command the organization completely. The cadres believed that an invisible entity infiltrated the boss while he was imprisoned. They believed this because the boss stated that he himself was an invisible entity endowed with a 'will' that could pass from one to the other. It became lodged in the boss after entering him.

The army intelligence concentrated on two critical points: the tumor and the sketch drawn by the Boss while hallucinating. The tumor and self-transformation were positively correlated from a neurological standpoint. Depending on their location in the body, tumors have been shown in studies to send arbitrary signals to specific parts of the brain. This could elicit a specific reaction, resulting in a shift in the individual's behavior pattern and extraordinary self-transformation.

Of course, the cadres discovered no causal relationship between the two; rather, they believed the two were governed in parallel by some enigmatic overriding factor. That mysterious factor was nothing more than the nature of the boss's 'will.' It was incomprehensible. A portion of it shaped the boss's transformation, while the remainder became a tumor within the body. That was why the tumor was so sensitive to even the smallest stimulus.

The intelligence research unit was divided over the sketch drawn by the boss in hallucination. One school of thought held that the sketch drawn by the boss was purely a psychic manifestation of the vengeance he desired to enact on a key figure in the government. It appeared as a skull masking the face in a hallucination. The opposing argument was that the shade of the human figure in the sketch had a distinct authoritative gesture typical of party leaders, and the skull represented vicious power. According to them, a strong leader drove the entire group. The boss was a sham figure who carried out covert orders. The chief of army intelligence sided with the second group and tasked them with tracking down the leader and his connection with the boss.

Since the day the boss was released, the intelligence group had engaged experts in recreating human faces from rough sketches and had hundreds of possible results. The search for the leader began with those simulated results and has been ongoing for the past six years. Needless to say, the investigation was fruitless and was still ongoing. In the face of the research group's efforts, the party's cadres remained deafeningly silent, convinced that they were chasing a shadow.

The boss had never been seen in public in the previous six years. His speeches were taped and relayed to various sections of the group. Every movement and action of the organization to be followed was meticulously planned in the manner of a tremendously sophisticated organization. The army intelligence unit was taken aback by how the organizational structure worked. As a result, their hypothesis about the organization's strong leader grew stronger over time, resulting in a more intense search for the leader. Nonetheless, the cadres and the chief of the intelligence unit saw their efforts as something sandwiched between the failures behind them and the "zero" possibility beyond them.

Everything abruptly took an unprecedented turn. The boss was said to be in a coma, but this hadn't been officially confirmed. Some party cadres realized that the tumor within the boss's body had exploded, and he fell into a deep coma with no guarantee of regaining consciousness. Other members of the party ruled out such a possibility. They claimed that the tumor had preserved some of the 'will' and that the 'will' would only leave naturally. As a result, the tumor's explosion was ruled out. According to them, the boss wanted to delegate the 'will' to the second in command. He'd purposefully chosen a mysterious path that was beyond the comprehension of others. The army doctors supported the view that the tumor had exploded. In fact, according to them, it should have exploded long back, and the boss should have died much before. There was nothing odd about him dying. What was strange was that he had lived so long, and despite the explosion of the tumor, he was in a state of coma, not dead.

Even though the whole thing was suspected as a rumor, it triggered some immediate alerts within both cadres and the intelligence unit. The intelligence unit's chief summoned the head of the research group and gave him his mind.

"You don't have to speak if you don't want to," the chief said, "but you should listen carefully. Your six-year search resulted in nothing. I was ridiculed as much as you were. The army intelligence unit had pumped many resources into your hypothesis, which was only a hypothesis, nothing more than that. Now that the boss is presumably at his end, the natural leader must be in the close vicinity of the group. He should be finalizing the following phony figure. If you could not trace him now, you wouldn't ever be able to find him. I give you a month. For you and me, there is only whether you find him or not. There is no in-between. If you don't find him, you are simply finished."

Despite their differences of opinion on the subject, the two sections of cadres scrutinized a few senior party members. Speculations began among the cadres about who would be the next boss empowered with the 'will' of the invisible entity. The victor would almost certainly go underground. Yet, there remained some uncertainty as no one was sure if the 'will' would pass into some inconspicuous one. However, on one account, all the cadres settled. They were confident that the boss would not let the 'will' go until he found someone worthy of possessing it. Therefore, the possibility of the state of coma or hibernation continuing for an indefinite period could not be ruled out.

The time breezed by. There was neither any change in the status nor in the functioning of the organization. Every bit of a thing remained unchanged. The excitations gradually trailed off; the speculations tapered down, and the Boss in a coma became an accepted fact. After a month, the head of the intelligence research group called on the chief of the intelligence unit.

"On the last occasion, I did not speak because I did not want to," he began. I have a couple of things to say to you right now. First and foremost, I was unable to locate the leader. I'm not interested in debating whether it proves or disproves my hypothesis. However, it has no bearing on our coexistence with the group. If you look at the organization's history over the last six years, you will notice that it has been steadily growing. Then it hit a snag—a point of diminishing return. At this point, the presence of a strong leader behind the organization is unimportant. He did what he had to do, and he may have outlived

53

his usefulness. We now have access to all of the organization's cards; we know how they interact with one another, as well as their hideouts and a few double agents. Even if you are successful in locating the leader, it will be in vain. Leaders are born in the same way that you and I were. They, like you and me, can be replaced if we leave the scene." He continued, "Since I have utterly failed in my task, here is my resignation letter." The chief stared him straight in the face, making him feel like an empty pool.

Then, he broke his silence, "Do you mean to say I should resign? So far, two persons have been ridiculed: you and me. If you go, I'm sure there won't be a second idiot in your section who will take on the task of finding the leader. I'd be left alone to bear the brunt of the humiliation. You should do two things in this situation. First, stuff the letter into your pocket. And the second is that you should run for the goal, even if it turns out that there isn't one."

"Does it mean that the project is on for an indefinite period as the boss could remain in a coma for an indefinite period?" the head asked, shoving the letter into his pocket.

"It's time for you to go," the chief said, giving him a dirty look.

"As you please, sir," the head responded.

The head pondered a few things after leaving the chief's office. First, because the project would almost certainly continue indefinitely, he wouldn't have to be concerned about its accountability. His team would continue looking for the leader in the same way they had before. And he'd always have a report ready in his hand. Despite being on the opposing side, the boss undoubtedly offered him a prize. He should be grateful to the boss for this.

The second was a puzzling mystery and formed the core of the entire episode. The mystery squarely rested on top of a trilateral power base: the boss, the invisible entity, and the leader. If all three were real, the mystery could hardly be solved as it had a solid base. If the two were real, then it would also be hard to resolve. If one and only one were real and the rest were phony, as he hypothesized, the mystery could be cracked. But it did not turn out that way. Because the invisible entity cannot be chased, his team never attempted it. Because the boss is underground and not visible, the search for him is futile; and his team does not even try. The only thing that remained was to find the leader. His team had been working on it for the past six years with no success.

That brought him to a third point in the picture, which he considered to be an excellent possibility. All three power bases were most likely phony, and the boss's story was a blatant lie. This was a well-crafted behind-the-scenes story about the coexistence of the two sides, the party and the government, with honorable and intermittent clashes. Then, someone could have devised the entire scheme and created the story. And he was the genuine boss.

Work from Home—Online Office

The digital clock read six-thirty a.m.; the alarm was buzzing. Sany slipped out of the comforter and into the bathroom. He was out in half an hour, freshly shaved and bathed. He spent another ten minutes on the dressing. Then he went down to the dining table and drank a glass of orange juice and oat cereal with milk. Wookie was staring at him. He needed to eat breakfast at this time. Sany had just finished preparing his food and was about to present it to him when Salini appeared dressed. "Did you prepare his food from the left or the right can? On Thursday, it had to be from the right can."

"Don't worry, it's all recorded in the phone; there's no room for error."

Both arrived at the Metro station in less than fifteen minutes. They were on the platform after two and a half flights. The train was waiting for them to get off, as it were. The doors behind them closed as they stepped into the compartment. The train got started with a gentle jerk. Sany had to travel five stations, while Salni had to travel seven. The train compartment was deafeningly quiet. Everyone's attention was glued to WhatsApp. Faint smiles occasionally passed from one to the other in an unnatural rhythm.

"Bye, see you on the five-thirty p.m. train back home," Sany said to Salini. Sany climbed the elevator. After a ten-minute walk, he arrived at the office and entered his cabin precisely five minutes to eight. He placed the laptop on the table and his bag on the floor below.

Saba called out from her cabin, "Hello." In the same tone, he responded.

The computer screen showed three meetings before lunch and two after lunch. They will consume almost five hours of the day. Of the five, two are with the idiot boss. They'd be simply infuriating. The boss would make the meeting last as long as possible by pointing out flaws in everyone. The poor man was unable to complete his MBA. He had to abandon it halfway through and had since developed a strategy to cover it up by blaming others on topics he couldn't finish—a victim of an inferiority complex.

Wookie knocked on the door at noon, just in time for lunch. He usually had his lunch at the same time every day. Sany walked straight to the dining table after opening the door to his small office room in the house. Salini came after. "Give me fifteen minutes. I'm going to heat everything in the woven; I'm not going to make anything new." Meanwhile, Sanny prepared food for Wookie, who had it at 12.15 p.m. Sany and Salni discussed the pre-lunch office session while taking lunch. They both had nearly the same story to tell. Salinini's boss was even more of a moron than Sany's. Both finished their lunches on time with cups of coffee. Salini made the lunch ready for the two kids, who preferred to eat it at two p.m. They were working on their online classes in the basement.

The office doors slammed shut at one p.m. There were two meetings left. Sany decided to speak as little as possible during the first meeting as he felt dizzy. At the second meeting, the idiot would be present, and it would be preferable to gain energy before that by taking a pseudo-power nap. He was pretty much sure that everyone else was doing the same thing. As a result, the first meeting was essentially meaningless.

The idiot made elaborate points. It took more than an hour to complete. Sany responded to a few emails, finished some personal projects, and made a few phone calls as soon as it was over. The day had almost come to an end. He turned off the computer.

He grabbed the bag below and stuffed items to take home. He left the office, walked ten minutes to the metro station, and boarded the train. Salini stood in the train's compartment, one hand on the holding rod and the other on the mobile phone. "How was your day?" she inquired.

"Everything was fine except for that idiot," was the quick reply.

"The same here," Salini said.

They were home in fifteen minutes after a brisk walk down the clean road. Wookie was waiting for them at the door as lavender dusk settled over the small town.

The entire office work was scheduled online, with two mandatory video clips attached to the office computer system, one at the beginning and the other at the end. The office computer would not start without the display of the first video. And it would not shut down unless the second video finished. The management believed that the two videos played a critical role in maintaining a cognitive, physical presence in the office while not being factually there. It was essential to alleviate the anguish of being confined at home due to the Covid.

Love Resurrected

A friend of Raju called him up and informed him about the funeral. The friend gave him the details of the funeral, too, and said, "I think you are going to attend her funeral." Raju replied, "It had been a long time since she left me, I had no idea where she went and didn't even know her family lived here in this town," he continued, "Where and when did she die?"

"A remote place near Darjeeling on 8 July. The body was handed over to her family by a few of her friends," answered his friend.

Eight July, eight years before, had faded into a distant memory. *"I am going to live to be twenty-eight,"* she said, *"then die,"* flashed across the mind of Raju. Exactly eight years later, she was dead at twenty-eight.

On the day of the funeral, Raju took a car to reach the place his friend described. There were buses, taxis, and three-wheelers everywhere, each overlapping with the other causing utter chaos. The whole area was a maze of narrow and wide streets and side drains. Raju ended up lighting cigarettes one after another, asking for directions each time. Finally, he reached his destination. It was a small, ordinary house with a brown board around it. Her father, a short man in his mid-sixties, stood by the entrance and scarcely moved.

She had left home when she was eighteen. No one in her family was happy with her leaving the home. This might have been the reason why the funeral was attended by only a few family members who looked scarcely moved like her father. On leaving, Raj lowered his head in silence. Her father stood as he was without a word and did not show any sign of movement.

Raju met her ten years ago; he was twenty, and she was eighteen. There was a small tea shop near the university where Raju hung out with friends. It wasn't much of anything. A few benches spread around haphazardly. A small boy distributed tea to everyone. The owner, a middle-aged man, made the tea. The tea offered a special test that was used to draw the customers in plenty.

She would always be sitting in the same spot, the corner of a bench, with a book in her hand. She would like the tea to be cold and sip it as she flipped the pages of the book. The first time Raju spoke to her was about a book she held in her hand, and then, of course, the trading of books began. The friendship steadily grew over cups of tea. They would talk endlessly on any number of topics, go for walks in the nearby parks, and smoke cigarettes now and then.

She had several names, but she earned a fixed bad name, recalled Raju. She would go to the nightclub with anyone, and that's how she was known to her university friends—they would say, "Oh, that girl who would go to the nightclub with anyone!"

Once and only once, Raju asked her about the standards she maintained when choosing someone to go with. "Well, if you must know, she stared at him." A pensive minute went by, and then, she began, "It's not like anybody I am going to pick. There might be a standard in the back of my mind, but I want to know about a lot of different people. Or might be that's how my life is coming together for me."

"Has it helped you get a wider sense of people around you?" asked Raju.

"A little," she said.

Raju knew hardly anything about her background, nor did Raju ever ask her. In one of those endless talks in the parks, Raju came to know that she left the house because she couldn't adjust to others in the family. She wanted an independent life of her own with the freedom to do anything prompted by her impulses. Only one thing defied her impulses and was constant with her, and that was the book. She loved to read books on a variety of subjects. Once, she said, "My mother was a school teacher, and she always had a book in her hand. Like me, she also left the coop as she had a big falling out with my father." She didn't say the reason for the falling out.

She would sit mostly in the tea shop and hardly attend classes, drink cup after cup of tea, chain-smoke, and leaf through books. At the end of the day, she would leave with someone for the nightclub. Once, Raju asked her, "Why don't you attend the classes regularly?"

The Prompt was the reply, "They are so boring; teachers ought to have brought changes in their styles of teaching. The same note is taught every year in the same way."

Raju remarked, "The teachers also must be getting tired of teaching the same thing over the years. But how many sheds could one offer on the same subject?"

She answered, "That's their problem."

She hired a cheap studio apartment near the university campus as she disliked staying in the hostel. Now and then, on nights, she would invite Raju to her apartment. Both of them would cook a simple dinner and put it away with the radio-tuned full blast, fill the ashtray, and talk endlessly on a variety of topics till midnight when the air outside was filled with particles of silence. Sometimes, a startling white moon would glare through the window.

It was a bizarre night when Raju walked into her apartment for the first time. That evening, she was alone in the tea shop. Raju reached there by chance for a cup of tea. As she saw him, she said, "There is no one today to take me to the nightclub. Why don't you accompany me?"

Raju replied, "I am not a clubbing guy and have hardly spent any time in a nightclub."

She retorted, "That does not offer enough reason for not taking me to the nightclub, and nightclubs are, after all, a different variety of clubs only."

Raju stared her in the eyes and said, "I don't mind accompanying you if it makes you happy." Both of them started at the nightclub.

They occupied a table in the club. She ordered two bottles of beer and lit a cigarette. Raju looked around. The disco ball light that swirled above cast every hue of the rainbow into the darkness. The dance floor could hardly be seen; it was wall-to-wall, and people were dancing to the tune of music. Ready to step in with the music, they danced, one with the music, and one with the figures, dancing on the floor. The music was like a drug rambling everyone in that place. As he finished looking around, Raju took a sip of a beer from the bottle and lit a cigarette. She had finished her first cigarette and lit the second one. Raju asked, "What's next, then?"

She replied, "You be seated here. I shall join the crowd on the dance floor, dance as long as my feet carry me, take breaks anytime I feel thirsty to visit you and the beer. The waiters know me very well. You just order the beer you wish to drink and keep a few bottles for me. I shall visit you during breaks and quench my thrust."

"What about the smoke?" asked Raju.

"Cigarettes jump from the lips to the lips to the tune of music," she said and then disappeared into the crowd on the dance floor. She had three breaks, each time she bottomed up a bottle of beer, took the half-smoked cigarette from Raju, and finished it in three drags. She had sweats on her body, some of hers, some of the others. The tip of her nose was red and wide, her breaths were deep and heavy, and her vibes flowed with passion, but she looked happy and more alive.

At the end of the night, she and Raju were quite drunk. They left arm in arm wobbling down the lamp-lit street to hire a cab. They reached her apartment and together they fell into the bed. Raju's head was heavy. He fell asleep before she had time to get a little frisky.

The next day, as the morning stepped onto the noon they got up. She made two cups of coffee and browned five pieces of sausage. She took two; Raju took three. She rested one of her arms on the table, put her head on the arm, and was sipping the coffee slowly. A few streaks of hair curled onto her face covering a part of her eye. Suddenly, she gazed at Raju in the face; her eyes were too piercing. She said, "You are way too different from others."

Raju asked, "In what way?"

"That's for you to find out," she said.

Memories that faded further and further into the distance like displaced cells reeled back in Raju's mind on his way back home. They overcast his mind and then melted into a heavy downpour drenching him thoroughly. He utterly needed a shelter to protect him from the oppressive downpour. He asked the driver to stop the cab near a bar.

The bar was relatively empty. He chose a corner table and

ordered a whiskey on the rocks. He downed the glass into his throat, ordered for the next, and lit a cigarette. The tip of the cigarette cracked dryly as its smoke formed a trajectory in the air. He sized the cigarette to half in three drags and then gulped the next peg of whisky. His head was gradually getting empty with shapeless images drifting and diffusing. He ordered more whiskey and lit one cigarette after another. The diffused shapeless images reappeared and began taking shapes.

She said, "Let's go for a long walk today through the small forest unto the stream." They started walking with their hands in their pockets, crossed the main streets and alleys, walked over the wide field, and then entered the forest. The trees in the forest were rustling their leaves in the afternoon breeze. There was no other sound except the crunching of the dry leaves below their feet as they walked through the narrow passage in the forest. They looked up to get a glimpse of the sky through the openings of the leaves. The sky was blue with patches of light white clouds stooping over the forest. They walked in silence for a long while before they reached the edges of the forest.

Raju broke the silence, "You are unusually silent today. What are you brooding over?"

She replied, "There are many ways one can feel someone's presence. I was just feeling your presence in silence."

"You are in a bit philosophical mood today. I wish could make a vibe flow to break the silence of my presence," said Raju.

She laughed and retorted. "Try if you might but the flow will disappear in no time as it will wind through the endless rows of the tree."

As they crossed the forest, the stream was in view. They got down the slope, went close to the stream, took a handful of water, and splashed it on their face. Then they stretched on the grass looking upward. An array of skylarks made a full circle over the stream and landed on the tall trees on the other side of the stream. Then, they flew one by one and were swallowed up by the cloudless sky.

All of a sudden, she turned toward Raju and asked him, "Do you have dreams of flying in the sky?"

"No, I often have dreams of climbing up the mountains. While doing that, I tend to slip down quite often sending a chill through my nerves, and I wake up. You may call it a bad dream rather than just a dream," replied Raju.

She laughed and said, "You are very protective, like a mother."

"You seem to have studied a lot about dreams," responded Raju, and then, asked her, "What about you?"

She replied, "I mostly fly in my dream to unknown destinations, sometimes to nowhere, and hardly wish to come back."

"What does your study of dreams say about it?" asked Raju.

"It is simple, I don't want to be caged and wish to remain born free."

They spent a long while on the grass until the sun climbed down over the mountain. The time breezed by. Then, they got up, put their hands inside their pocket, and started moving toward the forest. The sound of the flowing stream gradually faded away behind them. They looked up. A flock of birds crossed the course of thin clouds on their way north. As they entered the forest, the sound of the wind hissed through the branches of the trees. They continued moving through the forest.

Raju wanted to come out of the oppressive memories. His head was heavy. He ordered for another drink, downed it through his throat, and then, lit a cigarette. The lavender traces of the

65

smoke spiraled in the air. Through those spirals, she came floating back again in his memory.

On one eerie evening, she had put the radio in full tune and filled the dining table with some dishes. Raju never saw her preparing more than one dish. She would prepare only one dish and Raju would prepare the other. That's how they used to have their dinner together. Raju was surprised as he entered her apartment. "What's the matter, is there anything special today?"

"No, I thought I shall give you surprises," she replied.

"Are there some more surprises awaiting," asked Raju.

"That's for you to find out," she said.

They finished the dishes one by one, emptied bottles of drink, filled the ashtray, and talked endlessly on any number of topics. Time was surely passing by and the night was getting denser. She rested her one arm on the table and was listening to Raju. Suddenly, she mid-swing the conversation and asked him, "Do you believe in ghosts?"

"Not in the least," answered Raju.

She began, "You know, my mom used to say her brother had entered my body after his death. From early on he was a restless guy, used to take up only risky jobs, and spent most nights in the nightclub. He never listened to any of the elders and led an almost a reckless life. Finally, he died young. Whenever I used to become restless or disagreed with elders or got into an adventurous mood, my mom would repeat her brother entering my body. Once I asked her if she meant what she said. She answered, 'Her grandmom and her grand-grand mom believed in such things. So, she also believed it unquestioned.'" Raju laughed out and said she might be joking with you.

"But is there anything wrong if I do believe what my mom believed?" she said.

"It is your wish," replied Raju. Silence hovered between them for a while.

Then she spoke up, "Aren't we getting too used to each other?"

Raju stared her in the face for some time and retorted, "We are used to leaving on this earth, but never spell it out. What's wrong with getting used to anyone or anything for that matter?"

She replied, "I am afraid, for what I do not know."

"There must be something in your mind that makes you afraid and there ought to be some reason for that thing to exist in your mind. If you might spell out the most obvious, you might as well try to speak out about what's not so obvious to me. A true friend is like a confession box of a church."

She suddenly embraced him for the first time since they met and said, "I don't want to leave you."

"All right, then, don't leave me," said Raju.

A pensive minute passed by before she uttered, "I don't wish to make your life troublesome. I am something of an authority on troublemaking. I can claim to be second to none in the ways and means of creating a problem for others."

"That's how life goes. Every family has some problem or the other. Problems drive the family, peace is a resort on the path," said Raju.

With a spoon, she started making some abstract figures on the table which were neither visible nor were they decipherable. Only she knew what she was drawing. She dropped the spoon on the table midway, gazed Raju in the eyes, and said, "I could not stay with my family, nor my mother could with hers. We were a kind of drifters."

"I am going to live to be twenty-eight," she said, "then, die like my uncle, and after my death," she continued, "I shall enter your body and live with you forever."

Raju smilingly responded, "Like your grand-grand mom would have said!"

The call of an early morning bird shot through the window. They didn't know when they went to bed and fell asleep.

Two days later, Raju went to the tea shop. Everything was like as it was before, except that she was not sitting in her place. Raju thought she must be busy elsewhere. She wasn't in her place the next day. He enquired with the tea shop owner. He crisply replied that she had not been coming for the last three to four days. Some kind of a chill passed through Raju. He rushed to her apartment. It was locked. He enquired with the owner of the apartment. He informed him she left the apartment four days back. It was the day after the night of their last dinner meeting. Raju plunked down on a nearby culvert. Gazed at her apartment vacantly. He felt a pang in his heart, an experience that he never had before. What twist of fate, what uncanny course of events brought him to face this pathos? Nearby, there was a cry, neither of a bird nor of an animal. He also cried. He never cried so much before.

The restaurant was closing down. The waiter approached Raju and offered his services to call a cab. Raju looked blankly at the waiter and said he would appreciate that. A few moments later, the waiter informed him that there was a cab waiting outside. He had a whiskey walk through the corridor. The waiter opened the gate of the restaurant for him and helped him to get into the cab. The driver asked for the address. Raju said something. He didn't know if it was the correct address. It was all left to the driver to do the rest of the job. The driver dropped him at the right place as Raju could feel the vibration of an old elevator, to which his nerves were all tuned, as he entered it. He waited for the elevator doors to open and then close behind him.

He gathered up the pieces of his mind to climb up the few steps to his apartment. His head was blank from the whiskey and his mouth reeking of cigarettes. He staggered on stairs, stopped in between, and finally planted himself in front of his doorknob. Then, he fished his keys out of the pocket and leaned forward, forehead against the door. Somewhere there was a click sound and the door was wide open. He fluttered his hand to find the switch. There was a mild sound and the room shone out of darkness into a glow.

She was slumped over the table, forehead on her arms, profile hidden by straight black hairs.

"You, huh?" exclaimed Raju. As expected, there was no reply. She could have been asleep, could have been crying, and could have been dead. It was a minute before she raised her head slowly, evenly, and gazed absently at the wall. Raju sat down opposite her and rubbed his eyes. The shadow of a table lamp hood divided the table; Raju was in the light, and she in the shadow. The colorless shadow showed up a few strands of her hair lay plastered against her dampened cheeks.

"Don't mind me," she said, "I didn't mean to cry. I just came to tell you, 'I am still in love with you, don't want to leave you and stay with you forever.'" Raju saw her get up from the table, and turn walk toward him through the alcoholic fog, finally disappearing in him.

Two years later, Ivan weaved through the boys and girls like a pro, his smile wider than the space between the ends of an arch bridge. He was the hero of the nightclub. He came down from the dance floor amid the cry-dance, dance, and dance. He sat down at a table and looked around. Nothing much had changed over the years. Even the table, where he used to sit, was standing there as before. The only thing that had changed was the name of Raju. He was known as Ivan, a popular name in the nightclub.

Sunni Baba
(Holy Man in Space)

Deng, as he was affectionately known by his friends, lived a long life. His parents gave him the name Deb Nath Ghose. However, his overabundance of popularity shortened his name to Deng. He was a wonderful person, a lovable man, and a helpful friend to all. After having a few girlfriends, he decided to remain single. He discovered that marriage was not a wise decision to live a happy life and he indeed led a fairly enjoyable life remaining single. Most of his friends left for heaven by the time he reached eight-five, leaving him almost alone. In the last leg of his journey, he was afflicted with a variety of ailments, particularly gastric syndrome. "Time does not forgive anyone; it only gives one what is owed to him," he realized. He was aware that the gastric disease did not kill anyone, but one might be enraged enough to wish for death at any time. He attempted suicide twice because the disease's torment was unbearable, but each time he failed. Maybe he didn't dare to die.

Finally, one inconspicuous evening, he was tortured unbearably by the devil, and he decided to end his life. "He's lived long enough on this planet," he reasoned, "it's pointless to give the devil more opportunities to bother him by extending his stay here." He drew his bed close to the window, climbed up it, and then took another step to stand on the window's ceiling. From there, he looked down. With the half-moon in the sky, everything below looked beautiful. The breeze was gentle, and the sky was stunningly clear, with stars twinkling in it. Suddenly, he was struck by how lovely the earth was. It would be a foolish act to say goodbye to it.

"*The earth had been so beautiful in the night whenever there was a moon in the sky,*" he heard a voice say from somewhere, "*you'd seen it many times before. The fear of death underscores what is now projected in your mind. It's either now or never if you fail to complete your mission by tonight.*" He immediately closed his eyes, made a move from the ceiling, and lost his balance. A complete blankness engulfed him.

He awoke, but where was he? "Where am I?" he voiced a question to himself, "Do I exist in this life?" He looked up. In the first rays of sunlight, the clear blue sky was visible. The sun had only risen a few degrees in the sky. The silence hung around everywhere, broken occasionally by the chimes of the birds. He had the impression he was lying flat on an air cushion. A thought flashed through his mind, "Am I floating in space?" He noticed a crow flying above his head. "Oh, venerable one!" he said to the crow, "could you, as the most knowledgeable being among the bird's clan, assist me?" The crow turned around, dived down, and made a smooth landing on his forehead.

"What's the problem?" Looking down into his eyes, the crow inquired.

He replied, "I am completely perplexed, so much so that I can't figure out where I am. Furthermore, I have no idea in which state I exist."

"You are caught between heaven and hell," the crow replied, "you have not accumulated enough points by performing good deeds in your life to be admitted to heaven. You haven't scored so low either to be sent to hell. In terms of your state, you're in a daze."

"Thank you for enlightening me," the man said, "but I'm too hungry. Can you help me in any way?"

"It's utterly satirical that God remains hungry with devotees offering sweats to Him," the crow said with a smile, "if you turn around and look down, you will see smokes of fire rising in the air from the location on earth that would be hit by a pendulum if it were tied to your body. The smoke is rising from the sacrificial fire that has been lit in your honor. There are a variety of sweets offered in your name, tagged as 'Sunni Baba,' the holy man in space. And you're lying helpless and hungry in space. I've never seen God so helpless."

The man replied, "I couldn't understand a single word you said. Could you please be more candid and clear, and bring me something to eat?"

"You were first discovered lying in space by a young boy in the early morning when he came out to the balcony to relieve his pressure," the crow began, "he immediately informed his family. They came to find you exactly as you are. The news spread like wildfire. By the time the sun could barely be seen in the sky, the location and surrounding areas had been swarmed by dozens of devotees. They began formal worship in your pet name, which they created. The municipal commissioner has been notified. He'd be there soon to decide how much of the space should be designated as a holy place. The devotees have already devised several plans to be implemented at that location."

Saying these, the crow was about to take off when the man pleaded, "Please get me something to eat."

"Let me see what I can do," the crow replied.

After a few moments, the crow reappeared, accompanied by two assistants. The two were holding two paper cups in their mouths, one containing two sweets and the other containing hot tea. The crow told the man to satisfy his hunger with the little food they had brought and would get him a good lunch. The crow added, "They will look after you, pointing to its two assistants. Call them whenever you need them. I will visit you whenever I have the opportunity and inform you of the events that have begun." The crow took off. He felt much better after finishing his breakfast and was able to feel his current existence. Autumn had arrived. The breeze was light. The sun's rays were soothing. More importantly, his gastric syndrome had significantly improved. It's possible that the clean air did the trick.

"There's no harm in staying like this until some other event changes the course of his fate," he reasoned.

"After all, he is currently being worshipped, which was furthest from his thought. Even if he does not physically meet his devotees, he communicates with them through their prayers. And they have elevated him to the rank of holy man. He closed his eyes with great satisfaction."

He opened his eyes when he again heard the crow. "It is lunchtime, and you're sleeping as yet," the crow said, "have your meal. It's fresh." The man noticed the two assistants with two cups in their mouths. He took them from their mouths, and to his utter surprise discovered that it was his favorite dish-rice mixed with cereal. This was a common offering in most worship, and devotees enjoyed eating it. Before leaving, the crow informed him that there had been little notable progress in the event. Only the commissioner had been to the site and approved their plans and activities. The visible change had been an increase in the crowd. The number of devotees who came to the site had multiplied many times over. The crowd appeared to be getting out of hand. The organizers had already set up a special line for the VIPs to use when visiting the location. Many dignitaries had already paid their respects. By the evening, some of the ministers were expected to pay their visits. For this, special preparations were being made.

He took a short nap after lunch. As the evening approached, he wished to enjoy the beauty of nature. He noticed the brushstroke reddish clouds in the sky as he looked up. The lavender dusk was setting in. In a short while, darkness covered every space as one blanket. The night was especially lovely with the appearance of the half-moon in the sky. The stars were twinkling across the expanse of sky that he could see. The weather was pleasant. He thought he'd be much better off here than at home. For the first time in a long time, he had a trouble-free evening; the devil didn't appear.

Before retiring to their nests, the two assistants brought him his evening meal. Before leaving they said, "We shall be taking the night's rest somewhere near to you. If you need us for anything, just give us a call." He finished his dinner. It was quite sumptuous like the lunch. The crow had made excellent arrangements for him. He was now certain that he did some good acts in his life even though he could not score very high to be admitted to heaven. Otherwise, one could hardly get such a good treatment. He told to himself that he should be content with what he had been granted.

He was not feeling sleepy. So, he looked at the moon and then shifted his gaze to the twinkling stars. He'd never paid such close attention to the twinkling stars before. The big stars were in positions in space that had been predetermined by someone as it were. No one had ever seen them with naked eyes to be hanging in space like a huge ball. Only the eyes of scientific reasoning had witnessed them and convinced everyone that it was the reality. The other reality was the twinkling stars visible in the sky with the naked eyes. Both realities existed for the same object! It is as enigmatic as his current existence. Many more amusing experiences occupied his mind until they faded into obscurity; and he dozed off.

It was late in the morning when he opened his eyes. The two assistants approached him and stated that they had previously visited him. They didn't wake him up because he was sleeping. They would get him breakfast now that he was awake. The man finished his breakfast and thanked them for their generosity. "You are our honored guest in space," they replied, "we should look after you. We don't get human beings free in space very often. Those who are found, are either buggy jumpers or mountain fliers. They only stay in space for a short while."

The crow arrived during lunch and inquired as to how his previous night had gone. "First and foremost, I must thank you for the excellent arrangement you made for me," the man replied, "the last night went off without a hitch. I was enjoying my current stay far more than I did at home. I may wish to remain here indefinitely."

The crow stated, "There have been quite a few developments of the event. The organizers have formed barricaded queues to manage the crowds. The location is open for visitors from eight o'clock in the morning until midnight. A local decorator has created an appealing temple out of local materials. It's been beautifully decorated. A few stores have sprung up, selling lockets and rings emblazoned with the 'Sunni Baba' emblem. They are being sold as if they were cakes. The shopkeepers hope to start selling the prayer booklets with a short biography of 'Sunni Baba' by tomorrow. The majority of political party leaders have visited the site. Rumor has it that only a few of the political party's leaders, who are non-believers, are also willing to visit the site. Some preparations are underway to make this possible without tarnishing their image." After the briefing, the crow flew away.

He was pleased with the news. Finally, near the end of his life, he rose to prominence, though not in his name, but by the name devotees attached to him. He thought, *After all, the person is the same no matter what name he is given.* His thoughts continued, *Even though he has been denied entry into heaven, the comforts he is enjoying can be easily classified as second-tier. So, he must have been perched quite high above hell. A sigh of contentment filled his mind once more.*

The crow returned the next day around lunchtime and inquired about his well-being. Then the crow began, "There has been significant progress in the events at the site. Everything is, of course, on the bright side. The prayer books are now available in stores. The shop counters are extremely crowded. A few agents have taken advantage of this opportunity to sell the books at twice the price. The same is true for lockets and rings. The organizers have also begun the process of recycling the offerings. The vast majority of the fruits are returned to the fruit market at a discounted rate. Sweet boxes are being offered closed so that they can be resold to the sweet shops. The organizers have begun to amass a sizable fortune. I must say that you are truly assisting a few people to be prosperous. It would undoubtedly help you earn more points. Who knows, by the time the events take on a larger scale, you'll be elevated to heaven? Nonbelievers had also paid a secret visit to the site just before dawn when there was no one around. After reviewing the organizers' activity plan, they appear to have supported the cause. So, have a good time, and congrats on becoming famous."

Except for the overwhelming increase in devotees, several

uneventful days passed. During this period, the municipal authorities joined hands with the organizers. They began releasing sanctioned plans for the construction that would begin on the site. Money was being transferred from one side to the other. It appeared that construction would begin within a few days.

While the flag of 'Sunni Baba' was flying high, the number of devotees in the temples surrounding the region had trailed off to a bare minimum. Some of the temples were nearly deserted. The majority of devotees migrated and sought refuge under the protection of 'Sunni Baba.' The temple authorities were under a lot of pressure. If the current continued to flow in the same direction, their business would be forced to close. This necessitated immediate action on their part. Despite their differences, it brought all of the temple priests under one roof. The temple priests decided to hold a round table discussion to come up with a viable solution.

The meeting was planned in secret in the largest temple. It was presided over by the temple's senior priest. He said in his opening speech, "We have met here at a time of extreme crisis brought about by 'Sunni Baba.' It is an unprecedented situation that we have ever encountered. We had our fair share of followers. The devotees were loyal and truthful to their chosen gods. They had never strayed from their commitment under any circumstances. For the first time, devotees were dissuaded in this way. I'm just wondering if it's the spiritual power of 'Sunni Baba' that's causing such a massive devotional drain, or if it's some other powerful politics at work. I've been associated with many famous holy men in my life, including my father. They drew devotees with their charismatic personality and mystic power. The more mystic powers they possessed, the more devotees they attracted. My father taught me everything he knew. I've inherited some of his abilities. But I'd never seen anyone with the kind of mystic power that can keep one afloat in space. This is incredible. I don't find faults with the devotees. In such a situation, they are bound to be drawn to 'Sunni Baba.' Regardless of what is in front of us or what is happening, each of us should think deeply about the crisis at hand and come up with a solution."

Other priests present at the meeting agreed with the senior priest's point of view. They were all excited about the prospect of devising a way to stop the devotional drain at any cost. A few of them pledged to use their spiritual powers collectively to tear down 'Sunni Baba's' power. Finally, it was agreed that they would meet again in a week. Meanwhile, every effort will be made to develop a concrete proposal to address the situation. It would be greatly appreciated if the collective spiritual power could be used to annihilate the power of 'Sunni baba.' Everyone went back to their temples full of hope and energy.

The days whizzed by. The sites' construction had begun. The main temple was designed to not obstruct the view of the temporary temple built on the site by the local decorator. The visits to the temple site had been planned more methodically. Each activity had to follow a set of rules. Discounted provisions were made for special offerings and sacrificial fires. The organizers were having a great time. Sunni baba, on the other hand, got used to his daily routine. The crow and its two assistants were watching over him as before.

The priests reconvened a week later in the same manner as before. Everyone was gloomy. The collective spiritual power used to destroy 'Sunni Baba's power did not work. The majority of the priests were unable to come up with a concrete idea. There were only four proposals up for debate. The first proposal was to approach the municipality and request that the work at the site is halted, claiming that the balance of different beliefs within a community would be greatly disrupted if 'Sunni Baba' was given such a great honor. The proposal was met with criticism. It was argued that the municipal authority had no say over the gods chosen by devotees. 'Sunni Baba' had a large following because the devotees had chosen him as their God. Furthermore, the municipal authorities had previously collaborated with the organizers. As a result, they would oppose the proposal. The second proposal was to bribe shopkeepers to stop selling the locket, ring, and booklet, and to spread the rumor that those involved in the sale of these items faced unexpected adversities. This proposal was also criticized on two counts. To begin with, a large sum of money had to be raised for bribery. Second, the shop owners were already enchanted by 'Sunni Baba.' They would be afraid to oppose Him. The third proposal was to send a few hard-core temple devotees to infiltrate the mainstream devotees of 'Sunni Baba' and spread rumors about his infamous life before becoming the holy man. Even now, he had appeared with some magical ability to amass wealth while using the organizers as a scapegoat. This proposal did not go over well and was rejected. The last proposal was drawn along violent lines. According to it, an attempt would be made, with the assistance of trusted temple followers, to incite mass violence to deter devotees from visiting the site. It was also rejected by the majority of the meeting's attendees. They wanted to avoid any violence. If it went the other way, they would be in danger because their followers had been reduced to a bare minimum.

The meeting hall was deafeningly quiet. The senior priest rose from his seat and began strolling back and forth in a thoughtful gesture. The lines on his brow became more defined. He returned to his chair after a while and broke the silence, "History of religion is dotted with fights between God men and even between gods. Humans, God men, and gods all have a desire for supremacy. Fights of various kinds have been observed since time immemorial. The weapons used in those battles were spectacular. In the fights, everything from the highest form of power, spiritual power, to the lowest form, muscle power, had been used. And as long as the two are fighting, the adage 'there is nothing wrong with love and war' holds. Either we or 'Sunni Baba' exist. It would be a fight for survival. We all have one goal in mind: to dethrone 'Sunni Baba.' If he is not present, his supremacy is also absent. I am sure you understand what I mean."

A brief period of silence ensued, followed by a chorus of voices asking, "How do we get rid of him?" They elaborated that during the day, it wouldn't be possible. At night, there would be tight security in the place. Furthermore, 'Sunni Baba' had occupied a high spot in the space, difficult to reach. The senior most priest put an end to everyone's queries by declaring he had a plan and all he needed were six men with good stone throwing ability. Even though they were all taken aback, they immediately offered to assist him with whatever he required. Everyone was overjoyed when the chief priest revealed his plan.

When the crow found out about the entire plan, he was saddened that such a heinous thing was about to occur. He began to think about how he could convey the message to 'Sunni Baba.' Finally, he decided to convey it directly to 'Sunni Baba' after much deliberation with his two assistants. *Let him use his mind to protect himself,* the crow thought, *he has seen more of life than anyone else involved in the scheme. Perhaps, he'll come up with a brilliant idea.*

The crow arrived the next day after 'Sunni Baba' had finished his lunch. "I have some bad news for you," the crow said.

"What?" he inquired quickly.

"For quite some time, the plan was being hatched," the crow began, "but I didn't inform you until it took a concrete shape. Now that everything has been finalized, I thought I'd let you know. As your popularity grew, the heads of all temples surrounding the region were threatened with extinction. All those temple devotees were drawn to you for no fault of yours. A natural shift in loyalty occurred, and those temples were abandoned. The heads of the temples gathered to find a way to continue their existence, and they eventually decided to eliminate you. You would no longer be having fun in space. If you are not present, the devotees will return to their respective temples!"

"How are they going to get rid of me?" The man was desperate.

"In a very brutal way that I could never imagine," the crow replied, "they intend to stone you to death three days from now, on the new moon night at midnight."

"Oh my God! I never imagined my life would end in this way. The most primitive method of killing a man is stoning. It is a heinous act unbefitting of temple priests. There are countless ways to murder a man. They could have used another method to end my life. I don't mind phasing out, but not like this. It's even more shocking than going to hell," he retorted and then exclaimed, "Oh, my dear friend! Did I do so bad deeds in my life that I deserved a position even lower than hell? Please do something to protect me."

"I am just an ordinary bird," the crow replied. "How can I go toe-to-toe with a human? I assumed you'd come up with a strategy to protect yourself. After all, you have a long life experience and have been through many ups and downs. I informed you of the bad news in advance so that you could protect yourself. There are still three days remaining. I am confident that you will come up with an idea that will help you defeat their plan. I am always available to assist you if you require it."

"Let me think about it," the man said after closing his eyes for a moment, "please visit me on and off over the next three days. If an idea occurs to me, I will discuss it with you right away." Every moment of the following days weighed heavily on him. The more he thought about the crisis, the more perplexed he became. He was terrified every time he imagined himself being stoned to death. He became hopeless on the last day and informed the crow that he had resigned himself to fate, "Whatever will be, will be."

"Let me see if I can do something," the crow said, looking at his condition.

The chief priest chose three strategically placed tall buildings near the site where 'Sunni Baba' was floating in space. He directed his men to carry six gunny bags full of stones onto the terraces of the buildings, two bags on each terrace. He instructed them to complete the task quietly so that no one in the building would be aware of it. Then, according to the plan, six expert stone throwers were hired, two on each building terrace, to complete the final task. They would take up their positions at eleven p.m. and wait until midnight to begin their actions. Three powerful searchlights would accompany them to focus the lights on 'Sunni Baba' when the action would begin. This arrangement was devised to ensure that no stone would miss the target. The entire scheme had been communicated to the executors by the evening.

Suddenly, a few senior priests, particularly those who had attempted to demolish 'Sunni Baba's power, approached the chief priest and expressed their concerns. They stated, "Since the collective spiritual powers of several priests were unable to destroy the spiritual power of 'Sunni Baba,' it is likely that he commands great power. He may have already learned about the plan to kill him using his own spiritual power. As a result, he could be shielding himself by erecting an invisible barrier around himself that no stone could penetrate. The stones would be reflected or deflected tangentially across the screen. Our entire effort would be in vain. What should our strategy be in the face of that possibility?"

The chief priest patiently listened to them before retorting, "If he is all that powerful, we have only one way out: to take refuge in him. We'd all become his devotees, return to the temples, and replace our God statues with his emblem."

The day was like a slow-motion video that ended in the twilight for 'Sunni Baba.' The sky's lead grey gradually blended with black, eventually blending into night. The crow's two assistants arrived just in time for the evening meal. Sunni Baba was not in the mood to eat. He had completely forgotten about his hunger. He didn't even feel thirsty. "Miracles do happen," the two assistants said, realizing his condition, "don't be too upset. Consume something. You'd feel better. It is critical to keep your spirit alive until the end; you know this better than we do. We can only ask you to take some food and water."

He looked at the two assistants for a moment before taking some food from them and quenching his thirst with water. "We will stay very close to you."

The two assistants assured him. "Don't think you're on your

own."

It was the night of the new moon. The only thing visible in the sky were the stars. The darkness was deathly absolute beneath the sky. He couldn't tell the difference between one shape and another. He couldn't even see his own body. He could only surmise that he was floating in a vast black vacuum. He was reduced to a mere concept, as it were, that was only concerned about the impending danger. However, the passage of time continued unabated across the dark space.

The nearby church clock abruptly announced eleven p.m. He shivered; there was still an hour to go. Hundreds of events in the universe could occur within this one hour. But there was one and only one thing that was certain to happen: time would trail off to his death. Every second of the hour weighed heavily on him. He felt he was sandwiched between everything behind him and a zero beyond him, that he was an ephemeral existence with no chance or possibility.

The church's clock announced midnight. His heartbeats were as quick as the ding-dong bell. The bell stopped at twelve. Immediately, piercing rays of light shone down on him. Before he could realize what was going on, a stone flew past his left ear at the speed of a bullet. Another stone landed on his toe. He closed his eyes because he was afraid of seeing the stones slamming into him. Suddenly, a cacophony of a hundred crows' cries filled the air. Every building in the neighborhood had its windows open. Occupants were peering out the windows to find out what was causing the cries. The searchlights were immediately switched off. He was no longer being struck by any other stone. He was completely dazed by the incident and lost his ability to think. He became engulfed by emptiness and fell under a spell.

When he regained his awareness, he found himself lying on his bed with his two legs resting on the window's ceiling. A crow sat on the window panel's top edge, staring at him intently. "There are symbolic dreams that represent a reality, and there are realities that represent a dream." He needed to specify what they were.

The Shadow of Truth

The man with a grey overcoat took his chair and looked at Vishal without saying even a word. He didn't seem to be sizing him up, nor was his a pointed stare to bore him right through. He was just looking at him. He picked up a cigarette from the packet, lit it, and blew out the smoke upward. Then he crossed his legs. His eyes had a faint touch of blue; the two eyeballs were not at the center of the eyes and were, as if, focused in two different directions.

"Everyone dies," started the man and continued, "all of us will die sometime." The man fell into a long silence. There was only a buzzing sound of some unknown flying species outside. After a while, he started, "Let me have a frank conversation with you," he continued, "speaking frankly does not mean I am speaking the truth right away, or you would do that. In a discussion like the one which will follow, the frank statements will appear first, and the truth will appear last. The interval between them varies in proportion to the length of the subject." He continued to speak, "You are probably wondering why I begin the conversation like this. To dispel your muddle, let me show you this news item." He pulled out a piece of a folded newsletter from his pocket, put it on the table, and asked, "Did you print this newsletter?"

Vishal replied, "That is right."

"Did you get the approval of the authority before printing it?"

"I am not sure; sometimes, there are lapses. We print many newsletters on a typical day. It is hard to keep a check on each of them," replied Vishal.

"I am sure you are aware of the loss that you are going to incur for this. If you don't, let me tell you that you might lose your entire business, which you run in partnership with a big company."

Vishal looked at the man for a while and then admitted that he was pretty well aware of it.

"Excellent," continued the man, "In the line of your business, a small mistake could become the cause of a big risk, and precisely, you made that mistake."

Vishal took a while to size up the entire incident taking place in front of him. Then, he said, "So long has it been your turn to talk and question? Now, it's mine. Let me first assume that I had lost my business. With that in mind, can I ask who you are? And before you answer that, tell me who are you talking to?"

The man replied, "Two excellent questions, and I shall love to answer them. Let me answer what you want me to answer first." He continued, "There is no other person here besides you and me. So, your first question is redundant. But you might have a curl in your perception." That said, "He pulled his two eyeballs at the center of his eyes like a magician, stared at him through the nose, and released the eyeballs to go back to their positions."

He said, "I suppose your perception is now straightened out. As for the second question, I have to ask you something before I give you the answer."

"Did you ever meet the chief of the company with whom you have the partnership?" asked the man.

Vishal replied, "Not so far."

The man started, "If you enter his chamber, you will notice

four framed photographs hanging in a row on the wall. You must be wondering why the same four photographs are set like that. This thought will flash across your mind for no fault of yours. The fault is with the gene of the family to which the chief belongs. If you start from the right, the first photograph is of the present chief. The next one is his father, the third one is his grandfather, and the last one is the founder of the company and happened to be the grand-grandfather of the chief. All photographs were taken at the age of thirty-five when they were in office." He paused for a few moments and then pulled out a photograph from his pocket and handed it over to Vishal. Vishal's gaze got fixed on the picture for a long time, and then he stared at the man on his face. Before Vishal could utter a word, the man spoke up, "I could be any one of the four on whom your gaze was fixed. It should not matter much whether I am the past or the present chief. It is only the course of time that decides who is chief at what time. The fact of the matter is that the chiefs look the same, the past or the present chief."

Vishal replied, "Of course, it does not matter much to me as I have assumed I had lost my business. The only troublesome part of your statement is that one must believe in a ghost if you are the past chief. And the person showed up in the rightmost photograph is the only living entity."

The man pulled a cigarette out of the packet, lit it and blew out the smoke upward, as before, and said, "You are just at the right point." He opened the piece of the newsletter he had shown to Vishal and pointed his finger to a picture in it. It was some advertisement. A rookie reporter, fresh out of college, might have shown it in the newsletter—nothing extraordinary, four people entering a restaurant bearing the advertisement of a few food items. One of the four persons was marked with a circle. His finger was straight, pointing to that mark on the picture. He said, "The man in the picture with the circle mark on him died a few days before the picture was taken. That's what exactly gives credence to your statement you just made a few minutes ago."

A brief silence ensued. Vishal broke the silence, "How are you so sure that the man died before the photograph was taken? More importantly, what's the proof that this man was dead? And finally, who is that guy?"

He replied, "The man was an underworld businessman and made several attempts to destroy our business; you might call him our business enemy. Police investigations are underway regarding his death. Since he was known to be our business enemy, the police had already made two visits to our main office. Quite likely, they might visit your printing unit too. As to your first question, the answer might be hard to believe, but it is as sure as the man's death." That said, he took a gun out of the pocket of his overcoat, pointed it at Vishal, and said, "I shot him dead four days before the photograph was taken."

For a while, Vishal had nothing to say except staring at him. Then, gathering up his pieces of mind, he said, "You made two more things very certain, too. A ghost can shoot a man to disappear from the world, and the man can reappear in a picture after few days. I must congratulate the gene of the family to which the chief of the company belongs for being so highly imaginative, not less imaginative than writers."

The man put the gun back into his pocket, lit another cigarette, blew out the smoke, and said, "As I said before, the truth comes out last. Writers are indeed very imaginative. But you and your partner friend are no less imaginative than writers. If I am not mistaken, you both started your career as a translator and then tried your luck as a reporter. You had been doing well for quite some time and took a step forward to become a writer. You both wrote a few short stories. None of them could hit the market. You made a wise decision to stop writing and move into the printing business. There you had plenty of opportunities to read a host of stories before they were printed and wandered in the continent of imagination as much as you wished. Matured in imagining events, you decided to start writing again."

Suddenly, there was a knock on the door. The man said, "Your friend may have arrived." Vishal got up and walked to the door. As he opened it, his friend Kedar entered the room. Vishal locked the door, turned back, and to his utter surprise, found that the chair on which the man was sitting was empty. He stared at his friend first and then looked around. The only thing that he saw was the half-smoked cigarette in the ashtray tracing a trajectory in the breeze. He rushed to the toilet and shouted, "Hey, is there anyone inside?" There was no reply. He walked inside the bathroom and found no sign of any kind of human occupation.

As he came out, his friend asked, "What's wrong? Why are you looking so tense?" Vishal plunked down on a chair and looked blankly at his friend. A silence hovered between them before Kedar spoke, "What're all these about? Tell me why you look so perturbed." Vishal slowly and steadily narrated the entire episode to his friend. The whole while Vishal was describing the episode, Kedar stared at his friend, astonished. Even after Vishal had finished, he stared at Vishal without comment for a while. Then, he spoke up, "If anyone else had narrated it, I would have thought he was under the spell of a daydream or a fantasy. Although it has been difficult for me to believe what you said; I have to go by faith in you and the smoke of a cigarette tracing a trajectory in space. To my understanding, the vanishing man could at best be a magician who is capable of pulling his two eyeballs at the center of his eyes." Time was indeed passing by, but they both sat quietly for a long time, imagining several possibilities.

At long last, Kedar said, "Before we come to a definite conclusion about what happened, we should do some homework."

The next day, they reached the main office of their tie-up company and walked straight to the person who cleared the news items before they were printed.

As they entered his chamber, he said, "Hey, what's up? Do you need clearance of news items?"

Vishal replied, "Not on this visit. This time we have come for a different reason." They took seats in front of him. As he stared at them, Vishal showed him the concerned newsletter and asked him whether he could remember if they had taken his permission to print it. Without looking at it, he replied, "All news items are shown to be cleared in my record, whether you show them to me or not. If I don't, my job is at risk." Having said that, he offered a big smile.

Kedar opened the newsletter on his desk and drew his attention to the picture in it. The person frowned at him for a moment, then opened a drawer and brought out the same picture. After a brief pause, he said, "The police had visited this office in connection with the picture, more precisely in connection with the murder of the encircled man in the picture. The man was known to be an arch-rival of our company and ran a chain of underworld businesses. He wanted to turn our chain of business into that of an underworld one," he continued, "don't worry about the police investigations. They are not going to bother you. They would revisit this office when the chief comes back."

Vishal asked quickly, "Where is your chief?"

"He has been on a business trip for the last fifteen days," said the person. It was a great surprise for Vishal! There couldn't have been more of a surprise for him. He looked at the person on his face for some time and asked if he could visit the chief's chamber. The man said, "Why not?" He took both Vishal and Kedar to the chief's cabin. As they walked inside, they saw those four photographs hanging on the wall—the same man in the same pose appearing in the four—an ever so curious thing to witness.

Back in their own office, they sat face-to-face across the table, where the chief left his smoked cigarette butts in the ashtray. They stared at the ashtray blankly. A world of fantasy floated between them. They didn't know how long they were sitting like that.

At long last, Kedar began, "Some things are now clear after we visited the company's main office. First of all, we don't have to worry about the newsletter's publication with that picture in it, nor do we have to worry about losing our business. Second, the investigations by the police are not of any concern to us. Finally and most significantly, the person circled in the picture had died. Besides, two mysteries have unfolded before us. First, a man dies before his live picture is taken, and the second, the chief, who is on a business trip, has a long conversation with you. We need not take any action on the obvious facts that have been revealed. As for the two mysteries, we can hardly do anything about them except fold them up and let them fade away with time."

Vishal said, "I cannot add anything to what you have already said. The only thing that bothers me is how the chief might know that we want to start writing again. We are certainly in good shape with the publishing work and will be happy to continue to do so. But to be honest, an underlying desire to become writers didn't disappear from our minds despite our past failures. On the contrary, the desire has been flared by the opportunities to get across others' writings that we publish. Since we cannot do anything about what has already happened, I have a proposal. It is a proposal only. If we begin writing again, why not make this event as a point to start with?"

Kedar stared at Vishal for a while and then responded, "Not a bad proposal. If we are going to have to start writing again, we have to start from somewhere. It could be very well a beginning. Tell me, how do we get started?"

Vishal replied, "You make a beginning from any part of the incident and carry it further until you want me to take it over and bring it to an end."

"That sounds good," said Kedar.

On one inconspicuous evening, Kedar made a beginning, "Police investigations revealed that the man in the picture was big underworld don. He ran away from home at the age of sixteen. He tried out several businesses but did not succeed in any. Finally, he got into the business of trading illegal arms. The person who brought him into the business was a deadly shooter who had lost one arm in an unfortunate shooting incident. Although the person killed his opponents in that incident; he had to lose one of his arms. He could still shoot four people with his only arm at one time.

After entering the business, the man wanted to train himself in shooting and became the disciple of the great shooter who was the business's boss. Soon he became the most favorite disciple and most trustworthy man in running the boss's business. He helped the boss to build a strong underworld kingdom. He pulled everything into it. Narcotics, arms, printing of notes, duplicate goods, liquors, all sorts of things that one could dream of. He also built up an extensive network of contacts in politics, finance, media, bureaucracy, culture, and law. He made sure that their businesses never faced any difficulty. At some stage of the business growth, the boss, recognizing his remarkable potential, stepped down to make him the business's boss. He, too, had not let down the hopes of his boss and had taken the business to a great height.

The chief was no less a proficient person in business. He inherited a large business empire and managed it with great competence. The business chain encompassed a wide range of businesses, starting from fashion dresses to automobiles. From the outset, the company was recognized for its sophisticated and modern style of operation.

There was no rivalry between the chief and the don in the beginning. Each was preoccupied with growing his own business. The first time they clashed was in the stock market over the purchase of a large number of shares. The don shifted his interest into capturing the chief's business units using his muscles in the stock market. Chief, too had a stronghold in the stock market as his significant revenue was derived from it. A bitter fight ensued between the two. The don was up in tarnishing the chief's business chain's image. The chief left no stone unturned to expose the illegal aspects of dawn's business. The conflict between the two heated up.

At the height of the conflict, a new front of the battle opened. It was centered on a woman, a well-known model in the town. She stood five feet, eight inches tall, and had a lovely figure. Her hair was blonde, her eyes blue, and her skin was red and white. Her brows were more expansive than an arch bridge. She made good contacts in the fashion industry and began to establish connections among the reach. Only then did the two rivals enter her life. She gradually drew them in with her enchantment. Chief was fascinated by her extraordinary expressive and vocal abilities. The don was captivated by her eagerness and support for underworld activities. Soon they formed a perfect love triangle. Time passed by, but the presence of a second man in the triangle was becoming a stumbling block.

She once said, "You're both my best friends, and I love you both." Neither the chief nor the don was swayed by her enticing words. She was left with no choice but to pick one and only one. That was never her intention. She needed the two top-reach persons on her side. She was more concerned with her position and money than with anything else. As a result, she got into the dilemma of whom to choose between the two. The only way out of the situation was to take a neutral stance; let the two rivals fight, and let one make way for the other. And she did just that. The unavoidable happened.

The showdown succeeded. Don challenged the chief to a gunfight. At that point, a third man appeared unexpectedly on the scene. He worked on low-budget films as a producer, director, and actor. It was unclear what his relationship was with the model. He approached the chief with a proposal to finance a film and requested the dawn to be a co-financier. He promised massive success for the film and significant returns on their investments in the future. Both were in a fix because they had not anticipated such an easy opportunity to invest in the film industry coming their way. They had been thinking about doing it for a long time but hadn't gotten the proper chance. With the prospect of a gunfight looming in the background, they agreed to fund the film. They regarded it as a business risk. Success would result in a double return, while failure would result in a no-return exit from the world.

The don was confident of victory because his master had trained him to shoot so well that he could take at least two people at one time. He wondered if he hadn't gotten a better deal before. The chief, on the other hand, saw the agreement as a calculated risk. He believed that his genre was well-versed in the art of shooting. His grandfather was a well-known shooter during his era. As a result, his chances of losing the battle were fifty-fifty, as the underworld don could be just as good at shooting as him. He thought that the risk of this nature was not uncommon in business.

A few days before the showdown, the producer solicited both parties' feedback on the best time to begin filming. The chief didn't have a choice, and neither did the don. The producer took this to his advantage. He put forward a proposal before them. Because it was merely a proposal, he said, they could refuse it if they so wished. Having said that, he proposed a live shooting of the gun dual as the first shooting of the film. Both stared at him in the face for a while and then agreed to his proposal. The producer expressed gratitude for their bravery and courtesy. He claimed that just this rare live shot would bring in so much money at the box office that it would be more than double the film's revenue. Both of them could hardly offer a better response to it than to simply stare at him in awe and admiration.

The location of the gunfight was chosen by the producer. It was a little way out of town, by the side of a riverbank. The town and the river were separated by a small forest. One bank of the river extended to the forest's edge, and it was overgrown with sparse tall grasses. The sky loomed large over the other bank. Three people walked through the woods to reach the river bank on the day of the gunfight. The producer positioned the camera at a location and peeped through the lenses to determine the two competitors' best positions.

The gunfight took place in the evening. In the near-dusk breeze, the trees in the forest rustled their leaves. The sky was feathered with a few white brushstroke clouds. Pale lavender dusk had settled over the river's entire stretch of water and banks.

The producer captured the two rivals in the sky's silhouette through the camera lens and then abruptly raised his hand. The piercing sounds of two bullets split the air. After that, only the particles of silence floated in the air.

Kedar had stopped writing at this point. He went over what he had written and was disappointed in his mediocre imagination. He thought that all of his reading stories had been in vain. It did not affect his writing at all. He approached Vishal and stated, "As you requested, I have completed my portion of the writing to the best of my ability. Unfortunately, the entire exercise was futile. There couldn't have been worse writing than what I've done— the same old story of two rivals, a love triangle, and a fight. I'm just fading up with myself. You'd better take over and finish it reasonably well."

Vishal stared at him for a while and retorted, "The world itself is so mediocre that you are mediocre as such. About that, there is no mistake. The world is dotted with only a few genii who shouldered the entire civilization to its current state. There is nothing to be upset about what you have written; I can say it, even without reading it. The story of rivals, love triangles, and battles is a timeless one for the human race. It will never come to an end. Only the color may vary. I take what you've written and do my best to give it a satisfying conclusion. Finally, if both of us discover it to be trash, there is no shortage of trashcans."

Vishal took the story further, "The gunfight and the shooting went to oblivion. The producer was busy with filming. The model was engaged in furthering her career and contacts. The businesses of the two rivals were running smoothly. It appeared as if nothing happened in between. The police visited the chief's office once more and informed the officials that they were searching for the chief who had gone on a business trip. The officials told the police that they had hardly seen the chief working in the office. He operated from somewhere not known to them from the very beginning. However, his all instructions were methodically passed on to every level. They were accustomed to this mode of operation. One more crucial point they revealed to the police was that it was strict instruction from higher-ups to say always that he was on a business trip when questioned. The police were pleased with the outcome of the investigation and asked the officials to continue the practice.

The police also went to don's business units. They discovered similar information when they inquired: the don, after taking over the business, became invisible, operated from a location unknown to the workers, and his instructions were meticulously passed on to them. The police officers returned silently.

The town's activities kept on moving as before except for two differences. The model went on to become the most popular actress in the film industry. She was the constant actress in films made by the same producer who shot the rare scene of a live gun duel on the river bank. Another significant change was that the police investigations came to a halt.

Vishal finished the story at this point and showed it to Kedar. After reading the story, Kedar remarked, "Mediocrity takes many forms. The story bears a witness to this. The reader is left to wonder who is more mediocre, you or me."

Vishal retorted, "On the contrary, the readers would be delighted to read a story that just fits into the definition of the short story that ends, but does not appear to have ended." It leaves readers with many unanswered questions, concerns, and possibilities. To wit, what was the outcome of the gunfight? So what happened next? What was the producer's relationship with the model? How did the two different business chains operate so smoothly despite the absence of one or both rivals? What was more important, who was the chief? Finally, why did the police investigation come to a halt? The inquiries raise a slew of possibilities. Readers would be left to speculate."

"As a reader, could you spell out a few possibilities?" Kedar asked.

Vishal responded, "There are several possibilities, and it is difficult to list them all. I just sketch a scenario that answers many questions."

He continued, "In the gunfight, both were injured and unconscious but did not die. The producer brought them and secretly treated them at his home. They came back to their senses, all right but were paralyzed. They had no choice but to get into the wheelchair. The producer made excellent plans for them to have the best life possible. He gradually drew them into his web and began running their businesses on their behalf. No one outside could even get a glimmer of it.

The model fulfilled her dream. She amassed enormous wealth and fame through the producer with whom she had a secret relationship from the very beginning. Both came to the town empty-handed to make a career. They had nothing with them except ambition and looks. Finally, fortune was on their side.

Although no one could have predicted the entire plot, the

police had a hunch. They interrogated the producer and the model and learned everything. Then, the cops made a secret deal with them."

Vishal paused for a moment and continued, "What I told answers most questions of the reader. But one thing remained still a mystery: who was the chief having a conversation with me in our office?"

"The plot that you have sketched is obvious and straightforward," Kedar said after listening to him, "There is no twist to it. Readers will not get a kick out of speculating on them. More importantly, it demonstrates the writers' inability to weave the plot into the story in an interesting manner. Finally, the reader's interest is not sustained by the presentation style. I have two suggestions. One option, of course, is to toss the story in the garbage can. The other option is to publish it and then stop writing stories in the future."

Vishal had been listening to him. The entire time, his gaze fixed on Kedar, not even blinking. After Kedar finished, he said, "There are plenty of examples in history where the third attempt met with success. I disagree with your decision to stop writing, but I wholeheartedly support its publication. Finally, I'd like to draw your attention to one of the story's strengths: stories are rarely co-authored."

Kedar said, "Let us, for the time being, agree on publishing the story. Let the course of events decide whether or not we continue to write."

"Excellent," replied Vishal.

The story was published. It didn't get much attention because no one talked about it. Kedar and Vishal were not upset about the expected outcome, but they had both stopped writing. They carried on with their printing business as usual. After about three months, a black-suited man entered their office and sat in the chair where the chief had taken his seat. He crossed his legs, drew a cigarette from the packet, lit it, and blew the smoke upward. He looked at them and said, "I liked your story. It has all of the elements needed to be made into a film. If both of you agree, we can enter into a contract to make a film based on the story's plot. To make a hit film, the scriptwriter would make a few changes here and there. You must give consent to that."

Kedar and Vishal couldn't believe it was true. They both stared at the man's face for a long time, a little longer than it ought to have been. Finally, Kedar stated, "It's a surprise for us. We assumed that no one would be interested in the story. We're glad it interested you and made you think to make a film out of it. We are delighted that you are willing to take a risk in making the story into a film. Your proposal is completely acceptable to us."

"I am a producer, just like the one you portrayed in the story," the man said, "I look for stories with the makings of a film. As I previously stated, your story contains all of these elements. Most importantly, many of the story's images are in our archive. The film will take at most six months to complete. As a result, your story has enormous commercial value to me."

The film was released exactly six months later. It was a huge box-office success. Kedar and Vishal both rose to prominence as writers overnight. A co-authored story had never been adapted into a film before.

Vishal offered Kedar a triumphant look and was about to spill out something. Kedar said with a calm demeanor, "Let us not waste time-fighting over the merit of the story. Remember, we are now branded. Henceforth, whatever we write will hit the market. They will sell like branded items. More importantly, we don't need to be concerned about the readers. Once you've been branded, readers will find meaning and beauty in your story, even if it's a load of nonsense. Readers create writers; writers rarely create readers. Above all, remember, co-authored stories are uncommon."

Both of them resumed writing stories. Every single story was co-authored. They became the most popular writers in the town.

Two years later, the town's cultural society organized a function to honor them for their significant contribution to literature. The town hall was full. The stage was magnificently decorated. Vishal and Kedar sat in the front row with well-known members of the town. The producer and actress of the film, which was based on their story, entered the hall hand in hand. They approached the two writers and expressed their appreciation for writing a beautiful story for their film.

After the mayor's speech, Kedar and Vishal were requested to come to the stage to receive the honor. They stood in the middle of the stage. The audience clapped. Suddenly, the lights went off. A few rays of mobile lights were visible to dispel the darkness looming large over the big hall. In that very dim light, a shadow figured before Vishal and Kedar. It was the chief, who was dressed in the same brown coat. His two eyeballs were glowing, one focused on Vishal, the other on Kedar. In a low voice, he said, "Congratulations on becoming the town's famous writers," and then added, "as I said before, the truth comes last, but the truth is yet to come."

Vishal was about to ask, "Who you are? Where did you vanish on that day?" Suddenly, the lights were on. The hall came to glow from the darkness. Vishal and Kedar saw the producer of the film, with the plaques in his hand, standing in front of them.

The Dream

Anu has had dreams that are identical to reality since he was a child. They were more like true stories than dreams. But they were all filled with pain. He could recall every detail of them after waking up. It would have been easier if he could tell the difference and say, "*OK, this is a dream, and this isn't.*" This significantly jumbled his thoughts. He gradually lost his ability to distinguish between reality and dreams. His dreams were sometimes more real than reality. And his heart was heavy with grief over the people's plight.

Anu discussed it with his parents and elders. They stared at him blankly and maintained silence, more silence than it ought to be. Finally, one of the elders broke his silence, "I suggest you consult a psychiatrist or a neurologist." He continued, "Might be there is something wrong with the functioning of your brain." Anu listened to him quietly and nodded.

He made an appointment with a psychiatrist the next day. He told him everything he needed to know. The narration lasted about thirty minutes. The psychiatrist was staring him down the entire time. He didn't even blink once. After Anu finished, there was a brief pause between them. The psychiatrist then declared, "There are circumstances in which unreality concocts an impression that overwhelms reality. "Yours could be one of those cases. But, in my opinion, a more likely scenario is that you don't sleep at all. As you lay down on the bed, you plunge into an intense imagination and create a world of your own equally real as the one you see at the beginning of every day. As the spell of the vision ceases, you feel you were dreaming as it were." He continued, "Very probably, this is the reason why you remember every detail of it. Dreamworld events are elusive in nature, so you cannot remember all dream-world events. What you need is good sleep." He opened his drawer, took out a small bottle, handed it over to Anu, and said, "Take three pills every night before you go to bed."

Anu earnestly followed the instructions for a month. But his dreams continued. He visited different worlds and went beneath the earth where he saw species resembling distorted humans. Everywhere, he experienced the pervasive sufferings: sufferings of humans, sufferings of objects and species around him. He experienced oppression where the crying of the oppressed ones wounded his heart. He came across utter chaos where his soul yearned for peace and order. Everything was so realistic to him that whenever he saw the war on the screen or violence on the street, he used to scream, "Oh, why do the people wish to bring suffering to them?"

He experienced happiness too in his dream world. But, they didn't last long, nor could they be contained for the longest while. Their impermanent nature was the result of ensuing sadness. All in all, what trailed off was the suffering.

After one whole month, Anu visited the psychiatrist to appraise his condition after he took the medication. The psychiatrist carefully listened to Anu and remarked, "Since you mention about two parallel worlds, a dream world, and a real world, both equally meaningful, I advise you to consult a neurologist." He continued, "The functioning of the neurons of the brain is not yet fully understood. It is the opinion of some neurologists that neurons duplicate their learning outcomes and preserve them in memory. Depending upon the state of existence, they might use one or the other stored in the memory, stamping the same impression in mind as that in another state of existence. Who knows if the neurons in your brain are working in the same way?" Anu lowered his head as a gesture of respect to the psychiatrist and said, "Thank you for everything. I shall follow your instruction."

Anu returned home and opened a science fiction book. He spent the majority of his daily time alone, reading. He enjoyed reading fantasy, comics, and cartoons in addition to science fiction. He also practiced writing. Because his dreams were narratives, he felt compelled to write them down and turn them into a book.

At dusk, Anu got up and went to his mother. Curiously, she looked at him. Anu told her about his meeting with the psychologist and sought her view on the matter. After a brief silence, his mother said softly, "Look, if you study your courses well, you will get good grades and also, get a good job. So, work hard for your courses like your other friends are doing. You don't have to go to a neurologist." Anu knew what his mother would advise. It was the usual thing parents say, but he was not particularly fond of going to the university or following regular coursework. No matter his mother's view, he thought he should meet the neurologist and finish the episode.

The next day, Anu went to a neurologist. His chamber was packed, not even a place to sit. He thought for a while about what to do. Another neurologist? But, he is the best in the town. So, he got into his chamber and went straight to the assistant sitting at the desk. Even without raising his head, the assistant spat out, "If any patient with an appointment doesn't turn up, I might give you a time at four p.m." Softly he replied, "Look, I am not a patient as such, but I need to talk to the doctor about some problem."

"Is it your problem?" asked the assistant. He nodded. "Then, you are counted as a patient, and you have to wait," said the assistant.

"Perhaps, you might be able to solve the problem. Can I share it with you?"

At that, he looked up and studied his face well. "Tell me your problem, but make it brief."

Anu started, "I have dreams which don't resemble dreams. They are more real than reality. That confuses me about the definition of reality. If the dream world is as real as the world we see with open eyes, then we live in two worlds, and there is no difference between the dream and the reality." As he was about to continue, the assistant signaled him to stop.

"I dealt with a similar case, but not the same as yours. The patient's dreams were like movies, flowed like a stream carrying all characters together, and had a solid theme and a clean finish. After waking up, he would remember them and could distinguish between the dream and the real world. His problem was with the sequence. If his sleep breaks, the dream also breaks. When the sleep resumes, the dream starts from where it trailed off. The senior doctor didn't interfere with my treatment as I could handle it myself. But your case is rather complicated by the presence of two worlds, and I suppose only the senior doctor would be able to solve your problem."

Finished with his talk, he got up from the desk and went inside the doctor's chamber. After a while, he came out, looked at Anu with a smile, and declared, "I made a special request to the doctor. He would see you after the next patient." With nothing else to do, Anu took a magazine from the shelf and started flipping through the pages.

After half an hour of waiting, he got a call from the doctor. He nodded to the assistant as he passed by him to enter the doctor's chamber. The doctor was of middle age with a few gray hairs scattered randomly over his head that offered him elegance in his look. As Anu neared him, he motioned his fingers for Anu to sit down on a chair in front of him. Then, the doctor stared him straight in the face for a brief while and asked him to describe his problem. Anu started briefing his situation, a bit more in detail than he did to the psychiatrist. The doctor was moving his fingers on the keyboard of his computer while he was listening to Anu. As he finished, the doctor looked at him and said, "As you were narrating your problem, I was searching for symptoms that match yours. Unfortunately, I found none. So, I have to ask you something more than what I gathered from you." He continued, "In the first place, do you think that you sleep while you are on the bed?" Anu gave him an affirmative nod.

"How do you know that you were sleeping?"

"I was not aware of this world. My dreams were connected to a different world."

"But that was a dream, not a reality."

"Not exactly. The things that I experienced were all real; they made the same sense and followed the same logical sequence that I experience when I am awake."

"Do you remember every bit of it after your dream is over?"

"Very much so."

The doctor studied his face well and then broke the silence, "A hypothesis and nothing more, the neurologists are now working on, is Neuro photocopying. It will take a long while before it gets accepted. Even if it does, it will do no good as no favorable treatment will come out. It will only help to explain certain uncanny functioning of the brain." He took a break and then continued, "It is postulated that some neurons of the brain photocopy their behavior. The neurons remain active when the brain remains awake. As the brain becomes passive, say during sleep or in a dream, the neuron's photocopies get activated. So, the existence of two parallel worlds for humans cannot be just ruled out. After all, the world is a creation of the brain only." A weighty silence ensued between them. Suddenly, the doctor got up from the chair, leaned over him, and said, "I suppose you form an excellent specimen for those neurologists who are working on this hypothesis. If you agree, it would be a pleasure to recommend you to a friend working on this subject. But, I have one element in your entire episode, which is not clear to me. That is about the sufferings of humans you feel so strongly inside you. It confuses me, but I am sure my friend will have an answer to it."

Anu got up from the chair and replied with total respect, "Thank you very much, sir, for your study and the time you spent on me. I shall get back to you as soon as I decide on your proposal." The doctor waved his hand as Anu left his chamber. He came out of his room. His problem remained unresolved. He hadn't the foggiest idea about what he was going to do next. He only knew that the sun would rise from one side of a featureless land, would shoot up in a cannonball arc across the sky, and then would sit on the other side. And his problem would remain unresolved.

He spent his days reading, as he had done previously. On one of those unnoticed days, his brother handed him a few books and said they were pretty good. A group of Buddhists published the books. He flipped through the book's pages. He jumped up, sat upright on the sofa, and stared transfixed at one of those books. *"This is exactly what he's been looking for!"* he thought.

The book explained how being "liberated" was the key to true happiness." There would be no more pain. What a wonderful thing it would be if happiness could last indefinitely. Not just for him, but for all of us. In that sense, he was captivated by the word "liberation."

After going through the books, he decided to join that group of Buddhists. On the first day, the master asked him why he wanted to join the group. Quietly, he answered that he wished to attain "Liberation and enlightenment." The master was surprised as most people wanted to join to improve their situation in the world or gain supernatural powers. The master was impressed with his answer and conversed with him on many topics for a long time. During the conversation, what Anu felt most was the effortlessness with which the flow of dialog went along and an underlying sense of calm, as if the air itself extended peace.

After joining the group, Anu worked there as a volunteer, office worker, cook, and perhaps, all sorts of things that one has to do in life. At the same time, he continued his ascetic practices. He was asked not to speak or think ill of others and not to pursue pleasure. There, he was faced with a strong contradiction. His friends would exactly do the opposite, and he felt that he was doing precisely the opposite of everyone else. As time passed by, he found university life pointless and lost interest in going to the university. He became a full-time member of the organization. He was sent for higher training for higher ascetic practices and was assigned branch activities. He took care of lay followers and those who lived at home and was also involved in office activities. The organization's founder often reminded everyone to "'put heart and soul into the work each was doing'." Though it was something boring for him to hear, now and then, such a meaningless repetition; he gradually found himself growing in knowledge. He could clearly understand the state of his attachment to various objects of the world. Day by day, he gathered more energy, sensed more detachment, and had more discoveries about his connection with the outer world. These discoveries were those of a third parallel world-a world that was much inside him.

While all these changes were taking place in him, his dreams raced with him. He dreamt as before. His 'so-called' second parallel world remained in the brain like the pictures in the celluloid. Despite his growing knowledge and sense of detachment, the suffering of life and the thought of the world's impermanence chased him like shadows. His friends advised him to take up intense, concentrated training to get out of his feelings.

He joined the intense meditation camp. It was a kind of extreme practice whose only purpose was to attain liberation. While doing this, lots of mystical experiences occurred to him. When enough of these took place, one day, he stood face to face with himself to find what he achieved. He discovered his mystic experiences were no more charming than the dreams that he had. They could not erase his feeling of the sufferings of life and the impermanent nature of the world from his mind. He thought as if his mystic experiences were standing as a veil separating him from the liberation.

He went to his master. The master looked at his eyes with extreme calmness. He felt as if everything in the universe had become motionless and quiet. Even his rambling thoughts were frozen. The master asked him to sit down on a chair. He plunked down in the chair in front of him and attempted to break the silence. He found his thoughts were not moving and did not know what he had to speak.

The master smiled at him and began, "Liberation cannot be

defined in words. Even if I arrange and rearrange my words, I would not be able to express the truth. When you are liberated, you would be above all suffering. You would only know a vast expanse of calmness, call it eternal peace or cosmic nothingness. No one has to tell you that you are liberated; you would know that you achieved it. You have to be patient and put your heart into extreme practice. Time does not move, but your mind does."

Anu listened to his master, and his talks made sense to him. But neither did he have an experience of calmness, nor could he come out of his dilemma. His dreams continued despite his intense ascetic practices and meditation. Only his inner world started becoming more real.

During this phase of ephemeral existence, he came across the book "Beyond Life and Death." As he turned over the pages of the book, he got fascinated by the word "Kundalini awakening" as he was fascinated by the name 'liberation'. He had no idea about what "Kundalini awakening" is, nor had he heard about it before. His immediate reaction was to know about it all. So, he started reading through every page of the book with deep interest. The book claims that through "Kundalini awakening," one can get liberation, and it can be achieved in three months. He wondered, "Is that possible?"

Anu already had good training in Yoga. It was no problem for him to begin the process. He did not require any guide or a master. Along with the dietary control, he followed the instructions in the book. Within a short while, he could effortlessly perform the practices prescribed in the book. He continued it for three months—never missed a day, every day rigor of four hours!

About two months into it, the base of his spine started to vibrate, an experience he had never had before. At first, he didn't believe it and took it as a psychological factor. The experience gradually turned into a feeling of solid warmth, like boiling water coiling up the spine to the brain. It wreaked havoc with the inside of the brain. He was dumbfounded. He ultimately experienced a different state when such an awakening happened. He felt something incredible happening inside his body; his brain started becoming lighter and lighter. He sensed as if he was floating in space. An experience of a peculiar world, perhaps an isolated world of nothingness, engulfed him.

According to the book, he reached the kundalini awakening and eventually got a state of liberation. But to him, it offered nothing more than discovering another world, equally authentic but equally transient. It lasted as long as he was in that state but broke as his dreams broke. Sure, the new experience offered him happiness akin to bliss. Still, it was not permanent, and the impermanence was the cause of his ensuing sadness. The long and short of it was that the suffering feeling did not vanish from his mind.

Anu was getting frustrated day by day as he felt he did not achieve liberation. He thought all his practices were of no use. Neither could they take away his feeling of suffering, nor could they offer him everlasting peace of mind. Sure, he achieved a relatively more calm state of mind and sensed a feeling of serenity, but they were as transient as his dream world. Nothing was permanent with him; nothing could offer him a sense of fulfilment. Gradually he embraced more loneliness and began visiting remote places in forests. There he would sit on the edge of a pool of water and gaze at the sky, perhaps, looking at nothing. Or else, he would sit under a tree with a twig in his hand, drawing abstract figures on the ground.

On one inconspicuous day, when Anu was sitting under a

tree and looking at the setting sun, a figure appeared from nowhere and stood in front of him. It was a human figure, a couple of inches shorter than him. The face was almost round, and the tip of the nose barely made a hump on the face. With two small round eyes and a wholly shaved head, the man resembled the laughing Buddha. The man stared him in the eyes for a while and then looked toward the setting sun.

"What do you think the distance would be between you and the sun?" asked the man. He frowned at him and said, "Why do you want to disturb me? I wish to be alone."

"I am sorry if I have disturbed you, but I came to take away your feeling of loneliness."

"How do you know I feel lonely?"

"The place where you are sitting and the object, to which you are looking, are both lonely."

"That does not prove I feel lonely."

"I am in complete agreement with you."

The man took a brief pause and then continued, "Frankly speaking, I wanted to drag you into a conversation. Now that we are into it let me go back to the silly question of the distance between you and the sun. What is your guess?"

"I don't have any idea. What's your guess?"

"It depends on what you like to hear. Distance is just a number measured on a scale. If you change the scale, the distance changes."

"You choose your scale."

"I don't have a scale of choice. If you wish to know the answer, it is zero. The sun is within your mind, and the mind can assume any dimension."

"On the contrary, the mind is just like a mirror. The world around us is reflected in that mirror. The sun that I see is merely

a reflection in that mirror. The sun is truly miles away from me."
He continued, "The world is very much real, and our minds
experience it in diverse ways."

While Anu was talking, the man sat in front of him, staring
him in the eyes. As he ended, the man asked him, "Why did you
stop? It is time for you to talk. I shall continue from where you
trail off when my turn comes."

There are many ways to make people talk. The man
persuaded him to speak by simply gazing him in the eyes. He felt
an impulse within him to spill everything out of his mind. He
continued talking about his dreams, different worlds that he
visited, sufferings that engulfed him, and the impermanence of
everything he felt every moment. He also spoke about how he
searched for liberation through ascetic practices to end his
sufferings and conversation with the master.

The man kept his eyes on him the whole while as he was
talking. As he finished, a brief silence ensued. Then, the man
broke the silence, "Let me begin from where you trailed off.
What your master said was right. The liberation can only be
realized, and when you are liberated, you will not have any
questions about its existence. But why do you seek liberation if
you are already liberated? Every soul is liberated, but he is not
aware of it. The ignorance covers his awareness. As the veil of
ignorance is removed, the liberation emanates of its own." He
continued, "The world that appears as real does not exist on its
own. The mind creates and sees it at the same time. It is a mystery
but true. The moving speed of the mind is faster than any
conceivable speed. So, our perception fails to recognize the
window of time between the creation and seeing." The man
stopped for a while and then, mid-swung the conversation, "If
you so wish, you may wander in the continent of arbitrary like a

blown-away leaf, sticking to nowhere. But your ignorance does not allow you to wander that way. You stick to everything you come across. When you look back, you find you have crossed a space in oblivion as it were. The objects, which appeared real and permanent to which you attached yourself, no more exist. They never existed. You created them in mind."

"But then, where does everything end? There must be an end to everything."

"Stop creating objects in mind. There would be no beginning, nor there be an end." The man continued, "You created any number of worlds in your dream. They were not permanent and were the causes of your suffering. As you stop creating, neither there would be sufferings, nor need you to be liberated."

"Mind cannot stop creating. As you said, it moves faster than anything else. How then, one can stop creating?"

"There are only two ways. Either kill the notion that you have a mind or let the mind create as it wishes. You remain just a passive observer."

As the man finished, a whirlpool of wind appeared from nowhere. Everything around Anu started moving in space. Dust spread all around. In the haze, he saw the man drifting away in the wind. In the growing distance, the man became a fuzzy dot, finally merging into nothingness.

After the storm was over, silence prevailed. But this was a different quality of silence altogether—a ponderous, oppressive silence. Anu's eyes closed down. He felt a serenity within, and then suddenly, in his mind, bloomed a lotus which grew bigger and bigger until it touched infinity and lost its form. It seemed he would lose his consciousness and identity. He never had such an experience before. He shuddered. An inner cry emerged from within to come back to his senses, and the mind came back floating again. But it was a different mind with a remarkable calmness that fortified his inner conviction that the mind never existed, yet it mystically did. He got up and started moving toward his home. Everything around him was the same as before, only he had changed.

Five Dollar Trip of SFO

Undecided on how to take the city tour, Vikash and Lokesh left the hotel in the morning. They walked down the sloping road to the park, which extended flat before the road sloped down again. They hovered around for a while to buy tickets to the city bus. They didn't find any but crashed into a genius who gave them a clue for a five-dollar trip to essential tourist spots of San Francisco. They boarded the bus to Pier 29, following his clue.

The bus departed from Crescent Square. They had two window seats to get a good view of the area. The bus speeded down the lane, leaving behind the city center. The skyline gradually shifted from skyscrapers to low-rise buildings. They went past malls, shopping arcades, theatres, and crowded areas of the city before reaching the seaside. The view shifted to isolated coffee shops, bars, tourist shops, and large piers along the seashore. The piers were numbered; Vikash began to count them. When the number was 29, Pier 27 cropped up. Lokesh remarked, "Your counting must have gone wrong; the piers look tricky; they can confuse anyone. Nonetheless, the final stop is pier 29. Everyone would get down there."

They got down at Pier 29, crossed the road, and headed for the seaside, walking through the deck that stretched to the seashore. On the deck, tourist shops lined up at different angles. The spaces inside were decorated with flowers, wooden crafts, and a variety of seating arrangements. The elevated footpaths, which crossed the lower deck, provided access to stores at the

117

upper deck. They both walked up the elevated path to the upper deck, peeped into a few stores, and came out in no time. Vikash said, "Too costly items, they are available at a much lower price in India." Lokesh nodded. After a quick stroll, they came down from the upper deck and headed to the edge of the lower deck, where the tourists crowded to get a glimpse of the sea. Vikash stood by the deck's railing looking at the sea and the Golden Gate Bridge.

The weather was fabulous. The Golden Gate Bridge, though it was at a far-off distance, looked clear. Kedar viewed the bridge from different angles. He thought, *According to the angle of view, the time of the day, and the beholder's frame of mind, an inert object can change its appearance like living things. Who says the inert objects don't have a life?*

Lokesh's thought was interrupted as Vikash exclaimed, "See how beautifu the Golden Gate Bridge's line diagram looks in space, not seen in any textbook. I wish I could show this diagram to the students!" Lokesh was not in a mood to answer him. He simply nodded.

"How about taking my photograph here?" asked Vikash.

"Sure," Lokesh took the mobile and was about to click when Vikash said, "Focus on me, don't focus on that bridge. Plenty of pictures of the Golden Gate Bridge are available on the internet."

It was only the beginning of a photographic session. Now and then, Vikash would fix himself on an object and ask for a photograph. Tired of clicking the mobile button, Lokesh asked, "How many photographs do you want to have?"

"I promised my daughter two hundred and fifty photographs," Vikash responded.

"All of yours?"

"Not exactly; they could be anything but worth being

photographed."

"Including yours?" Lokesh asked.

Vikash glared at him from the upper corner of his spectacle.

After an hour of wandering, they went to a fruit shop. Vikash bought some grapes and raspberries, gave half of them toLokesh and said, "We are going to finish our lunch with these fruits and have an early dinner; what your idea is?" Lokesh started him on the face. Vikash took a seat on a bench and asked Lokesh to sit next to him and said, "Think we were born in nineteenth-century Russia. You were Prince So-and-so, and I Count Such-and-such. We spent time together hunting, fighting, drinking, and being rivals in love. By the time your dream is over, you would finish the fruits and would be ready for the next move," he continued, "Is there anything left worth visiting here?" For the first time since they began their journey, Lokesh said, "No."

"Then, let us proceed to the Golden Gate Bridge," saidVikash. They started at the bus stop. It was located on one side of a big square where several roads had converged. Vikashasked Lokesh to follow him and then began crossing one street after another more randomly than the wind in the desert. He was as though drawn by the "walk sign" at the crossings. Lokesh quietly followed him. After crossing many roads, he stopped at the bus stop, looked at the signboard, and said, "We are at the right bus stop." Standing there, Lokesh looked at the opposite side of the road. All out there seemed to be familiar. He toldVikash, "Perhaps, we could have reached this place by simply crossing the road in front of us. Vikash had a look at the road and remarked, "Didn't you enjoy the adventurous road crossing at the famous Pier 29 square?" Lokesh responded, "Yeah, of course, it's easier to get the big things finished the hard way." Vikash looked at him again through the upper corner of his spectacle.

They took a bus to the Golden Gate Bridge from the bus stop and reached their destination in a short while. After stepping off the bus, they were lost among the visitors. Tourists were in different sites—on the seaside, on the bridge footpath, on the terrace garden, in the café, and on short trips across the bridge. Vikash stood by one of the tower's massive columns, moved his hands over the rivets, and said, "Hm, these are the real rivets, sunk so many years ago, still shining. This is called the wonder of engineering!" He took a few close photos of them and said, "These are exclusively for the students."

Lokesh looked up. The sky was appallingly clear, utterly cloudless. A helicopter flying high off in the distance looked minuscule. He began walking along the footpath to the center of the majestic bridge. The wind was high, but the view of the sea from the bridge was panoramic. Visitors switched on their cameras from the bridge deck to capture the Golden Gate Bridge visit's unforgettable moments in the celluloid. Lokesh stood passively watching them with their cameras.

When Lokesh returned, he found that Vikash had disappeared from the place where he had left him. He turned around and saw him taking a shot of another set of rivets. Lokesh said, "Are you short of two hundred and fifty photographs?"

Prompt was the reply, "I've finished the number. They're extras and not available on the internet."

They both walked around the tourist spots near the Golden Gate Bridge. Vikash went into most of the stores to have a look at the price tag. Lokesh was trailing him. After visiting the stores, they went to a coffee bar and ordered two cups of coffee. Lokesh said, "I suppose we're not just finishing our early dinner with coffee."

"This is a treat from my side," saidVikash, "After all, we should celebrate our visit to the Golden Gate Bridge, right?" Lokesh nodded. They spent a while in the coffee bar and then got up. Vikash said, "Well, it's time for us to return, isn't it? Lokesh said, "Time is one big cloth, no? We habitually cut out pieces of time to fit us." Vikash gave his typical look through specs. They started toward the bus stop.

As they boarded the bus, the driver stared at them. Vikash took two tickets out of his pocket and showed them to the driver.

"Put or don't put the coins in the machine, but don't show me the old tickets," the driver said.

Vikash put the tickets back in his pocket, thanked the driver with a smile, and got onto the bus.

Vikash took a seat by the side of the window, and Lokesh plumped down beside him.

"Keep an eye on the buildings," whisperedVikash, "I shall keep track of the crossings."

"Just for what?"

"Our destination is the landmark building at the crossing in Crescent Square," Vikash said in a low voice.

The bus ran along the two-lane route. The relentless procession of trees, footpaths, and buildings on both sides of the road seemed to decline faster than the bus's pace. Lokesh peeped through the trees to read the names of the buildings, then gave up.

"You can't read anything."

"Same here," responded Vikash.

Buildings and crossings passed by, each of them staring out the window with a blank expression. There were announcements on the bus as a stop approached; they didn't make much sense, as they weren't more than sounds to them. The two stopped thinking about their destination; they had no better choice. They thought, after all, that the bus would be coming back by the same route.

"Are the Tickets for the single journey or day passes?" Lokesh asked.

"Nothing of the sort is printed on the tickets. If we don't get off the bus, we don't have to reveal the tickets."

"Just great," Lokesh relaxed on the seat, and Vikash closed his eyes.

The bus stopped at a couple of stops. Passengers got off the bus, and new passengers got on board, but the two remained undisturbed as if they had nothing to do with the bus stops.

Suddenly, Vikash said, we have got to get down to the next station."

"How do you know that?"

"There was an announcement about it."

The bus had stopped. Both got down and looked at the buildings and the crossing.

"Not the right stop," Lokeh said.

Promptly they turned back to the driver and asked if it was crescent square.

"You guys, come up," he said.

They stepped onto the bus; the door closed behind them.

The bus started with a slut. Vikash caught hold of the nearest aid; Lokesh clung toVikash.

"Get down after three stops," the driver said. Vikash stared at him. The driver raised three fingers.

They got off the bus after three stops. Lokesh stared at the landmark building, and Vikash pointed his finger at Crescent Square.

"We're in the right place. See the tom-tom," saidVikash,

"I'm going to have a ride on the tom-tom, go up the slope to the top, and then come down."

"You might as well get down near the hotel. Why come down?" Lokesh said.

"That is a loss of money," Vikash responded.

Vikash coined the word "tom-tom" for a decorated tram with three compartments intended for a tourist ride. Tourists hanging on the side of the tram waved their hands as the tram slowly traveled up the sloping lane. The tram intrigued Vikash more than anything else. He would say "tom-tom" now and then and laugh in his usual style.

As they headed to their hotel, Vikash said, "It took only five dollars to finish the San Francisco city trip. Those tourists, sitting on the roof of the city tour buses, would be paying sixty dollars for the same trip, fools."

Lokesh replied, "The tourists would cover the whole city. They would drive up and down the steep lanes like a toy train trip in the children's park. They would enjoy sea views, meander through the skyscrapers, halt at historical places, and perhaps, end the tour at a musical place for dinner."

Vikash began to clarify, "Look, you can split the city trip into three parts; the Golden Gate Bridge, Pier 29, and the downtown. We've been to the Golden Gate Bridge and Pier 29; our hotel is in the center of downtown. The view of the sea and the dinner at the music venue are just peripheral. We also had a seaside view at Pier 29 and the Golden Gate Bridge and would have dinner at the Indian Restaurant at night. The place does not have music but has a lot of noise; after all, both are sounds only! Moreover, I shall have a ride on a tom-tom, which is the same as the journey on a toy train."

"Sounds good; we covered the major ones in five dollars;

that's a big achievement," Lokesh said.

"That man in the park was truly a genius," Vikash said.

"Which man?"

"The guy who gave us a clue for the five-dollar trip to the major attractions of the San Francisco,forgotten?"

"Not at all; sure, he's a genius; otherwise, we'd have been sitting on the roof of the city tour bus just like those fools."

They got back to the hotelLokesh had begun to arrange for a power nap. Vikash saw him do it quietly. Suddenly, he said, "Take your power nap; I'll be back soon." When Lokesh got up, he noticed that Vikash was snoring on the bed. There was a ticket to the tram on his side table. Kedar had to realize that Vikash had ended his much-loved tom-tom ride.

Getting out of bed, Lokesh opened the window. A cluster of skyscrapers glared through the glass. The city center looked gorgeous with dim pictures of artifacts outside as the sun set behind the hills. The street lights became brighter; the traffic signal started to shine, and the panoramic view extended all over.

At approximately seven, both started for the Indian Restaurant. Vikash said, "5 junctions, turn left and go down." When both took a left turn, it was up, not down. "We made a mistake in counting; maybe an extra small crossing slipped into counting," saidLokesh. They turned around and finally reached the restaurant. The manager waved his hand as they walked into the restaurant. The guy was from Punjab. Vikash waved him back.

It had been a busy restaurant. Most of the inhabitants were Indians and Pakistanis. Vikash went straight to the manager to get the order. Without listening to what he said, the manager got up and accompanied him to make a place for the two and vanished.

"Strange, he didn't care for the order," Vikash uttered. Lokesh replied, "Don't worry, the dinner might come as a surprise." Vikash was worried as the Restaurant was a popular non-veg joint. He was not sure if they were going to get anything worth eating. "If he surprised us with a roasted chicken, I would finish my dinner with a masala tea," saidVikash.

"I don't think he's going to be so cruel to you," Lokesh said. After a while, the waiter came up with two "Chana-Pindi-roti" dishes.

Vikash said, "Glossy! I was just looking for this dish and waved his hand to the manager."

He turned to Lokesh and said, "Chana is good for you. It is rich in protein and low in cholesterol. It guards against heart problems, and lastly, it doesn't taste bad."

Dinners made. Both headed toward the hotel. Outside, it was unexpectedly warm, and the sky was heavily overcast. A moist breeze was blowing in slow from the south. A sea scent mingled with a hint of rain. It seemed that it would rain any minute. When it did, it came in so delicate a drizzle that one couldn't tell if it was raining or not. They speeded up to reach the hotel before they got thoroughly wet. As they reached the hotel, the rain came down heavily. Lokesh stood behind the window of the hotel room. Through the neon signs of the building next door, a hundred thousand strands of rain sped earthward through a green glow from the hotel window. As he looked down, the rain seemed to pour straight into one fixed point on the ground. The rain kept falling until midnight.

The following day, when Lokesh got up, he found that Vikash was ready with his luggage. He said, "Come down to the breakfast room. I'm going to wait for you there."

After half an hour, Lokesh came down. Vikash had his last

bite of the sixth muffin; there were two empty milk bottles on the table. He looked at Lokesh and said, "I have finished my lunch here; I don't trust Air India. Even if they don't serve a meal of my choice, I should be fine." Before Lokesh could finish his breakfast, the pick-up van to the airport arrived. He left his breakfast halfway through and boarded the van. Vikash waved his hands to downtown San Francisco.

They had to stand in front of the Air India desk for a long time. At the check-in counter, Vikash noticed the luggage tag was labeled "SFO DEL." He stared atLokesh. The Prompt was the response, "SFO stands for San Francisco." Vikash laughed in his usual style.

AI 179 took off from SFO airport in time. Lokesh occupied a window seat, and Vikash sat next to him in the aisle seat. With his seat belt fastened tightly, Vikash relaxed on the seat and said, "So, we finished our SFO trip, coolly and solidly—all in five dollars and laughed in his usual style." Lokesh looked through the window. White patches of cloud flew by in the span of a hand from the window. Down below, the city of San Francisco was shrinking until it disappeared into space.

Salt Palace

From my hotel room window, I noticed a Land Rover parked below. The driver, a middle-aged man in an army shirt, and black trousers stood leisurely by the Land Rover. I locked my door and rode the elevator to the ground-floor office desk. The man at the desk informed me that my vehicle was waiting for me in the parking lot. "Is the Salt Palace a popular tourist attraction, and how long does it take to visit?" I asked, handing him my room key. "Whoever comes to this place pays a visit to the palace," the man replied, "It's perched atop a mountain. It is viewed by tourists from the flat top of a nearby mountain. There is no more road for the vehicle to travel up. On a clear day, the palace gleams in the sunlight, and tourists end their visit by zooming in from various angles. The visit takes about two to three hours to complete." "Has anyone ever been inside the palace?" I inquired. "No, not to the best of my knowledge. To reach the palace and enter it, one must first climb a steep hill. That could only be done by mountaineers. I've never heard of a mountaineer pulling this stunt."

I went to the parking lot and got into my vehicle. The driver started the vehicle and steadied the steering wheel as he navigated the bumps in the road. When he got to the highway, he relaxed, turned around, and asked me, "For the first time in this place?" I replied in the affirmative. "Everyone who comes here visits the salt palace. It is ranked third as a tourist destination. The first two are the open market, which covers approximately two square miles, and the Dragon's Lake. One can walk through them, go shopping, enjoy boating, and eat at restaurants. I'm curious about what kind of attraction the palace has to entice tourists! The palace can only be seen from afar. It doesn't look any better than snow-covered mountain peaks in clear weather."

I asked him how many times he'd taken tourists to the location. "Several times, not counted," he said, "the tourists take pictures, while I smoke and don't even look at the palace." "Have you ever been tempted to go up and enter the palace? I asked a question. "I am not a trained mountaineer as such," he replied, "However, I have done some mountaineering in my life. Do you have any mountaineering experience?" I replied, "No, but if the palace looks appealing, I might climb the steep hill and enter it. What about you?" "The palace never drew me in, he replied, "Maybe because I go quite so often there. You look at it today, and if you like it, we might come back to the spot early tomorrow and make an attempt to go up."

After a few miles of driving on the highway, the vehicle turned onto a narrow road. It was too bumpy. Now and then, the driver had to steady the steering wheel. After a while, the road began to climb a mountain. The speed of the vehicle slowed down and the driver started negotiating every turn of the snaky path. The driver took about an hour through sometimes bumpy, sometimes gravel roads to reach the mountain's top plateau, and parked his car there. The narrow road we'd come on trailed away behind us, an all too picturesque course of twists and turns. I got out of the car and straightened up. "Move ahead for about half a mile, you'll find the tourists zooming their cameras," the driver said as he showed me a path through the mountain's plateau, "Just get lost within them and you'll see and learn everything there is to know about the Salt Palace. I'll be waiting for you right here." Having said that, he drew a cigarette from his pack and lit it.

I started walking down the path until I got to the tourist spot. The driver was correct. Tourists flocked to the location. I just blended in with the crowd and directed my gaze in the direction that everyone else was looking. "Splendid," I said, my gaze fixed on the palace. "Indeed it is," the man next to me said. The palace was about a kilometer long and was mostly white with intermittent bands of pink and gray. White gleamed in the sun's rays, overshadowing other colors that appeared to have faded. The palace's skyline resembled a few vaults with their sides merging down with a straight-line contour. It is perched high on the crest of a steep hill. A cacophony of human sounds and the clicking sound of the camera filled the air. I stood there for a long time, frozen, before returning to the vehicle. Even though I had no formal mountaineering training, I decided to climb up the hill and enter the palace.

I expressed my wishes to the driver on the way back. He kept quiet for a while as he navigated the twists and turns. Then he turned to face me and said, "If you're serious, we'll have to start very early in the morning; bring some packed food and water, as well as some necessities to climb the steep hill. I'll take care of the latter while you look after the food." We left early the next morning for our destination. The weather was nice, there were few cars on the road, and almost no one was heading up the mountain. We arrived at the mountain's plateau in an hour.

The driver parked the car in a convenient location and walked with me to a vantage point from which the palace could be seen clearly. We sat down, opened the food pack, and began nibbling as we discussed how to get to the palace. The spot, where we were sitting, was on the edge of a slope that dropped nearly a kilometer before meeting a flat section. The flat ground covered a large area. The steep hill started from the other side of it. The hill looked sparsely forested and large stones could be seen protruding from its sloped body.

"I hope you won't have any trouble ambling down the slope," the driver said, "it's not a particularly difficult descent. Take your time and go at your own pace. Please disregard my presence. I'm going to get down in my way." We started descending. I took it easy and slid down slowly, while he went fast. I could feel he'd had some climbing experience which gave me a lot of confidence. I got to the flat ground in about thirty minutes. We both started walking across the flat ground to the opposite side from where the hill began to rise. As we got to the bottom of the hill, he looked up and said, "You have to be extremely careful climbing up the hill. I'll always be behind you. As far as possible, use the strong branches of the tree and protruding rocks to help you move up. Try not to look down. I may use the rope to climb up at times and demonstrate to you how to do so. Take a break if you're tired." Having said that, he motioned for me to go up and followed me.

The ascent of the hill began. In the beginning, every step I took was cautious, perhaps more cautious than it ought to have been. Gradually, my speed of going up increased, and I mastered negotiating high slopes with the help of nearby tree branches and the edges of stones. When I became tired, I rested on large flat surfaces. The driver quietly followed me, always keeping an eye on me. I looked back once, and only once. Immediately, he pointed his finger up the incline. It was indeed a tiring long journey. The palace seemed to rise in tandem with me. I doubted I'd make it to the palace before the sun reached its zenith. "Don't worry, climbing high slopes gives misleading notions." My friend could read my mind and frisked away my fear. "Just keep climbing and ignore the palace."

After about an hour of climbing, we came to a halt. In front of me appeared a nearly vertical stone wall with no holding on its body. The driver stared up, looking for something to wind his rope around. He moved sideways to hit his target, and he eventually discovered one. He made a hook in the rope and threw it up twice before he could get a firm grip on a protruding stone, like an expert mountaineer. Then, he demonstrated how to climb the wall using the hanging rope and asked me to do so first. I summoned all of my strength and courage to follow his instructions and ascended the ropeway, eventually reaching the cliff top. He yelled at me as I was about to look down from there. The sounds of his voice echoed in the air.

The palace was visible from the cliff's top. The size of the palace was enormous, which cannot be comprehended from the tourist spot. I sat on a flat piece of stone and stared at it; my eyes tracing the ends of the palace in vain. From where I was, I could see another kilometer of the hill's sloped body, with large stones and bushes, until it merged onto the flat plateau atop which the majestic palace was situated. We both took nearly a half-hour to get to the plateau and stood in front of the palace. It was glaring in the midday sun.

The palace had a grand entrance, but there was no opening anywhere. The entire palace appeared to be closed and airtight. We moved in both directions sideways. Nothing we could find that would allow us to enter the palace. In a fit of rage, I sat down on a stone and told the driver, "The entire effort of climbing the hill was for naught. From the tourist spot, the palace appeared picturesque, and it would have been better if we had returned from there only like other tourists. Now that we're atop the hill we have to make our way down the same, fully distressed!"

The driver hadn't given up hope. He persisted in his search for a way into the palace. After a while of searching, he too gave up and took a seat on a stone a few meters away from me. I stared vacantly at the palace for a long time and then got up to say goodbyes to the palace. I approached the grand entrance, touched its pillars, and moved forward to touch the vertical wall which ought to have been a door for entry. As I placed my hand on it, I heard a faint sound from somewhere; the wall cracked open, and both sides began to slide apart, allowing me to enter the palace. I was bewildered, and before I came back to my senses to call the driver, he was right behind me. From where he sat, he was watching everything that was happening.

We both entered the palace. As we stepped in, suddenly inside walls became dimly lit, with soft intermittent musical sounds filling the air. The entire scene turned into a mystical setup. We stood frozen inside the hall where we stepped in, listening to the intermittent musical sound. All of a sudden, we realized that the sounds had a distinct rhythmic voice telling us something. We intently listen to the rhythmic voice. It took a while before we could discover that the sound was welcoming us into the palace. As we both realized what the voice was saying, the musical sound changed. It relayed something else. Thus, one at a time, the musical sounds trained us to listen and understand what they conveyed. It was then our turn to speak. "Thank you for welcoming us and teaching us how to recognize your voice," we said politely. "We are indeed happy that a communication has been built up." The musical sound filled the air, "We have as many things to learn from you as you do from us."

We moved ahead. The dim light illuminated sections of the wall with each of our footsteps. The sounds of our steps reverberated as we walked through the large hall. After a while, the musical sound was back in the air. We didn't have any trouble understanding them. "Long ago, two persons like you visited the palace," it said, "they were here for a week. Before leaving, they said they would inform visitors that the white chunk of mass atop the hill was a palace made of salt rock." "How did you come to know that they spread the message?" we inquired. The musical sound relayed back. "Every day, we see people zooming on the palace and hear them say the salt palace."

"It appears that you can see and hear from a long distance, how far can your voice travel?" we inquired. "Certainly a good question," the musical sound replied, "our sound only travels within the palace, but we can see a long distance and hear the faintest sound. Looking down from the top of this hill, the city from which you came, appears to be a toy city for you. But, we can tell you the height of every building in the city. If we wish, we can also hear the sound of the car rolling down the road." We asked, "Can you listen to what couples whisper on their wedding night?" Wrinkling sounds appeared in the air like a naughty smile. We've never heard a naughtier smile than this before!

"Who said mountains and rocks don't have a life?" I heard someone say, "*Life is spread everywhere, in every nook and corner. All one has to do is feel it.*" It sounded so true to me. The musical sound returned. "*The entire universe is full of life.*" The walls appear to have read my mind, "*Life is not limited to humans. Different kinds of lives exist in different parts of the universe. Life, contrary to popular belief, does not have a single definition. How galaxies after galaxies are suspended in space, without colliding if they had no intelligence. And intelligence is intrinsic to all lives.*"

"Enough philosophy," I said, "we're getting hungry. Could

you please help us?" "Follow the dim light that travels before you through the walls," the music from the stone wall said. We followed it for a while until we came to an elliptical expanse. A dome covered the top of the space. I had seen many different types of domes in my life; some were made of concrete but looked like the sky, some were painted stones, and still, others were simply white marble. For the first time in my life, I saw a lash green dome laced with green creepers. Various types of delicious fruits dangled from the dome. They were easily accessible. We picked some fruits and ate them to the full of our satisfaction. We were thirsty and searching for water when we heard the sound of a nearby stream flowing. We followed the sound of water which led us to a wall's corner. A clear stream ran down the openings in the walls. We drank water to the full beam to quench our thirst. A few moments elapsed before our eyes closed. As we lay down on the floor, we slid into a deep slip.

We had no idea how long we had slept. We awoke feeling energized. We went to the wall's corner and splashed water on our faces and sprinkled it on our heads and other parts of our bodies. It offered us a relaxing feeling and we were ready for the next adventure. "Hope you are now fresh and ready to begin the conversation," the musical sound returned. As we said before, we wish to know many things from you as you do from us." "It appears you know everything there is to know about us. There would be hardly any new information that we can provide you. But we have a lot of things to gather from you. Tell us about this palace first," I said. The sound began, "As you walk down, you would come across one hall after another. They are all empty. After a while, you will be swallowed by nothing but emptiness. You would begin to wonder why such a magnificent palace was built atop the hill. Who lived in this palace once upon a time that might have been lost in history? In reality, it was empty from the beginning. No king had ever reigned here. It was our domain. We were our monarchs. It was never built stone by stone. It took on its form and became a natural gift. In this palace, we live our lives in our own unique way. This is not the only rock palace that exists on this planet. Many mountains are home to such palaces, large or small. The caves that sheltered humans during the Stone Age are the smallest variety."

"You are indeed your monarchs," I replied, "But don't you get tired of the palace's monotony? There is no variation, excitement, or movement. You're like frozen statues in time. We would have assumed you were lifeless stones if you hadn't shown us your life through light and sound. We are accustomed to feeling movement in our lives. Now that you've said life doesn't have a single definition, we have started reconsidering our wisdom." "We have movements, tiny movements in the form of waves that you cannot perceive. These tiny waves, when combined, have produced the musical sound you are hearing. We communicate with one another via tiny waves. Through the tiny waves, we express our emotions and feelings. We are ecstatic and then come crashing down with the help of the tiny waves. We also use the tiny waves to dance like you. Our life force is the tiny waves. We're curious if you've ever considered how you dance and talk. As we understand, you also use millions of those tiny waves and combine them to demonstrate your existence and life. When the waves combine, you lose sight of the tiny ones. You identify with the larger mixed waves. That is your ego at work. Humans are inherently proud of their existence because of their ego," the sound retorted.

"Indeed. We are proud of our existence and most of us do look down upon other existences of nature. However, there are also quite a few, philosophical ones, who view all existences with an equal eye. There are many religious ones, who even worship other existences of nature. Worshiping the rivers and some selected members of the animal kingdom is quite common among us. On this planet, we are a rather unusual species. We have many different types, but they all look like humans. Beyond any doubt, the majority of us take pride in ourselves. That is also the reason for our dominance over one another. Throughout history, we have fought many wars among ourselves to gain superiority. We have yearned for peace also. We enjoy playing the game of war and peace. We are, indeed, nature's funniest characters. Do you have squabbles among yourselves? Do you like and dislike each other?" I was curious.

"No, we have harmony," the sound responded, "we are content with what nature has bestowed on us. Some mountains are larger than others. But, they don't envy each other. Some mountains are beautiful at sunrise, some are beautiful at sunset, some glare in the midday sun. But they don't fight amongst themselves. You mentioned that we don't have visible movements. We'll tell you how to tune in to experience our movements, maybe, in the form of dance that you like most."

"That would be fantastic," I said, "but first, let us finish our meal. We're getting hungry." There was a lyrical sound that resembled a smile. "You are frequently hungry," it said, "we are delighted to have such visitors. We have an abundance of fruits, but no one to enjoy them. You don't have to return to the same dome where you had your previous meal. After three more halls, you'll come across another dome. Enjoy your meal there." We passed through three more halls before arriving at another elliptical expanse covered by a dome. It was not green but wore a wheat color. Fruits of various varieties were suspended from

136

the dome. We had never seen them. We tried them and they were delicious. We ate them to our hearts' content, drank water as we did before, and started feeling sleepy. "No, you can't sleep right now. Cross two more corridors to get to another hall. We'll show you how to tune yourself to feel the finest movements and experience a different world of motion," the sound said.

We passed through two more halls before arriving at a different type of hall. Each stone on the walls was an architectural piece. Their forms were beyond our imagination. None of the shapes belonged to humans. The 'dancing Shiva' was the closest human form we discovered. We were astounded to see a plethora of such a variety of forms and were standstill for a long while, staring at them. "Lie down on the edge of a wall, fix your ear on it, and try to feel the tiniest waves passing through the wall," the sound whispered. We followed the instructions. Nothing happened in the beginning. We were exhausted and were about to fall asleep when the miracle happened.

We entered into a magical world. To begin with, it was all in slow motion. The scattered artifacts began to move in a circle. Slowly, the motion increased and took on a speed pleasing to the eyes. Then each piece began to dance in its style, each distinct from the others, but all synchronized into a harmonious symphony. For a long while, we were fully absorbed in the rhythm.

Suddenly, the dancing pieces turned into motionless statues. We were perplexed as to how the tuning had been lost. Only the fragment of time that slipped behind us knew if there was at all any tuning to the feeble waves that passed through the wall, if there were at all any dances of the artifacts, or if everything was a dream.

"No, you weren't hallucinating. You were seeing our

movements through the lens of dance. Tuning had to come to an end, or you'd have turned into stones like us. We and you are from different worlds of motion. Nature maintains the appropriate motion for each object on this planet. As you said before, life is all about motion, and motion can be found everywhere in the form of waves, from small to large," the sound replied.

"You're a bit of a philosopher. You sprinkle philosophy in everything. Yes, we are all aware that nature keeps everything in this world in balance. However, nature need not be drawn into each topic of our discussion. We, humans, are engaged in a wide range of magical drama in real life, as well as in theatre and film. Compared to that, what we had witnessed was not that extraordinary. Our roadside magicians sometimes perform better than what you had shown," I retorted.

"You are correct. We could see many of your interesting dramas in real life and on stage right from here. Humans are excellent magicians and dramatists. So we didn't want to catch you off guard with the short film in motion. We just wanted to show you that we're not stationary," the sound responded.

"Many thanks for the short film showcasing your feeble movement. Could you show us something on a grand scale that humans have yet to perform?" I asked.

"Demonstrating something of that magnitude is difficult. However, you might be surprised to learn that, unlike humans, we don't have a better half. We are unique in that we do not require a pair of opposites to exist. We are a single independent entity," said the sound.

"Now you show your pride as we do," I said, "You want to show your self-sufficiency. True, you exist independently. However, that is how you have evolved in this world. The animal kingdom as a whole, including humans, has evolved differently than you. What we want to know is whether your life on Earth has a greater dimension than human life."

"Well, human intelligence is undoubtedly higher than that of any other creature on this planet," the sound responded, "and you are more adaptable than other creations. You are also imaginative. As a result, we are unable to demonstrate any intellectual dimension that is greater than yours. You must, however, admire our physical size, which is enormous by any standard," said the sound.

"There is no denying the fact. You have physical dimensions that no other person or animal can match. Your solitary stature is also impressive. Many great souls on Earth were drawn to your majestic stature and sought refuge in you to realize higher planes of existence," I replied, continuing, "we had discussions on a variety of topics that were both interesting and enlightening. We also learned a lot from you. The time we spent with you will live on in our memories as a treasure. Moreover, like the two men who visited you a long time ago, we will spread the Salt Palace's message of life. Thank you so much for making our stay so pleasant. We had no idea what we were getting ourselves into when we entered the palace. Now, we realize that we were in dreamland as it were."

There was silence for a while. There was no light either. We were surrounded by darkness. We didn't know what to do. We stared up at nothing, helpless as we were. A few tears—like drops of water—fell on us all at once. Surprising us, the sound returned with the beaming light. The sadness was audible in the sound. We could hear the rocks crying. I couldn't keep my emotions in check either. Tears welled up in my eyes. With a choking voice, I said, "We did not want to leave you. But we must leave. We are from another world. We can't stay here forever. We'd have had to leave sooner or later." "We don't get humans coming over here," a repentant voice replied, "but we had a great time after a long time apart. Your pleasant company relieved us of our loneliness. After you left, we would continue to live our lonely lives. Even though we are proud of our solitary existence, we envy your vibrant collective life. We are saddened by the prospect of parting. We understand, however, that you will have to part with us one day. Please continue to follow the light. It will take you to the exit." We followed the light back to where we started. We were both standing against the same wall. It creaked open, and the two sides slid apart to make room for us. As we walked out, we could hear a sad voice saying goodbye. "Bye," I replied. The two sliding sections of the wall closed behind us.

Painter's Village

One of Ananth's close friends invited him to the hills. His friend had built a nice villa there to oversee his business. When Ananth arrived in the mountains, he found his friend to be not there. He'd gone to the plains for an urgent job and would be back in a week. He made, of course, all arrangements for Ananth's stay in his home while he was away.

Three uneventful days passed for Ananth. Only the morning air of the pasture gradually turned cooler. As the first winds of the winter arrived, the bright golden leaves of the trees became more spotted. Killing time was not an easy job. So, he started to get up at six and jog a half circle around the pasture in front of the house. Stopping at its center, he could hear and feel the winds. They appeared to be saying, "There will be no turning back." The autumn had to give way and fade away into the distant past. For a passing time, he began cooking as well. He asked the cook to only assist him and get him what he needed. He cooked chicken. He defrosted the fish, marinated it, and browned it. They all tasted great with red wine. He would spend the majority of the afternoon gazing out over the pasture. When he looked out, the pasture in front of him used to gradually evaporate into oblivion. In its place, a figure emerged from the woods and ran straight to him. More often, it was one of his family members, but it could be a schoolmate or his friend. Other times, he discovered him to be wandering through a large mansion that he visited once. But, in the end, nothing lasted. It was all a daydream. The only thing that existed was the wind that blew across the pasture. It was as if the pasture were the winds' thoroughfare.

His friend returned on the seventh day. He was relieved to see Ananth in his home. He apologized for his absence, took a seat next to Ananth, and described the urgent task that he needed to complete. While talking, he asked the cook to bring two cups of coffee and some snacks. Sipping his coffee, he was about to describe how the weather in the mountains could change when suddenly the first snow fell. Since the morning, the winds had been unusually calm. The sky was obscured by dense grey clouds. The wind shifted suddenly, and the snow began to strike against the window panes in a series of dull thuds. The storm quickly intensified, and everything outside became awash in white. The entire mountain range and woods were shrouded in obscurity. "This is the real snow here. Everything is blanketed in snow, which freezes deep into the earth," his friend said. "How do people work in such weather?" Ananth inquired.

"Most of the time, the snow does not last long, and people get back to work within a few hours. However, on rare occasions, the snow continues to fall for hours and piles up. Returning to work takes two to three days. People here in the winter are accustomed to this way of life," his friend answered. Ananth saw the snow stopped falling by early afternoon, just as his friend had predicted. As the thick cloud in the sky ripped apart, the columns of sunlight thrust down to shine on the pasture. In a matter of minutes, the snow that appeared to defy melting had all but melted.

They had a lavish dinner that night. After dinner, they relaxed sitting in front of the fire with cups of coffee. While sipping his coffee, his friend told Ananth about his business and the various opportunities that Ananth could avail himself if he wished to start a good business. "Tomorrow, I shall take you on a tour of the places in the mountains where our people are at work. We could have breakfast together in the morning and then proceed for the tour," his friend said before retiring to bed.

The next morning, both of them were in a Jeep, driven by Ananth's friend. The road was jerky that wound through the mountain. It led them to a plateau at the mountain's summit. The road came to an end there. The jeep moved across the pasture, hitting a few bumps here and there. After about two kilometers of driving, the jeep came to a halt. It couldn't go any further. The terrain in front ambled down through the dense forest. They stepped out of the jeep and began descending the slope, carving a wavy path through the woods. It was an adventure for Ananth to travel down such a road. He had never done anything like it before. They remained silent and focused on the path ahead of them until they reached their destination.

Ananth was taken aback to see men in various groups failing trees. Each group was led by a leader who gave instructions. Two of the leaders came forward to greet them. Ananth's friend introduced him to those leaders. They showed Ananth all of the sites where the work was going on. One of the man asked him if he would like to see the place where the woods are rolled down to the plains in pieces. Ananth responded instantly, "I would love to visit the site very much." It was at the peak of the mountain. From there, a large area of land, completely razed, steeply descended. The logs, which had been cut into pieces and tied with rope, were gradually rolled down using pulleys mounted on the mountain's crest. Down below on the plains, logs were arranged in different groups and stacked in layers. They looked like children's toys from the top of the mountain.

Following their visit to the sites, Ananth and his friend

returned in the same way as they had come. Ananth's friend asked him to walk faster so that they could arrive home before sunset. Many thoughts raced through Ananth's mind on the way back home in the jeep. He had a lot to talk about with his friend during the relaxing moments after dinner.

Following dinner, they sat on couches in front of the fire. Ananth told his friend that he had an interesting tour experience and had a lot to know from him. His friend gave Ananth a long look before telling him to go ahead. "You know, I don't come from a business family," Ananth began, "the way the wood business is run was an eye-opening experience for me. But many other related things piqued my interest. To begin with, the men doing the work appeared to me to be a hilly tribe. I could understand what they were saying, but they had different accents. Their physical appearances attracted me the most. They were nearly six feet tall on average, with a muscular body, shining black hair, and a complexion that matched their hair color. Some of them had razor-sharp features. I was moved by their simplicity. How did you get them for your business? Where do they stay? How do they connect them to the people of the city? Do they have to travel to the plains to get their daily necessities? Do their children receive an education? Finally, how much money do they make and how much profit do you make from your business?"

His friend responded, "You asked a lot of questions. The majority of them, however, are linked to people who are at work. Let me try to give you some context for everything you've seen on your tour. That may provide answers to many of the questions you have. My father inherited a large portion of this mountain from my grandfather, along with other properties. You could refer to it as our ancestral property. My father had no intention of starting a woodworking business at first. We didn't need the mountain, and the mountain didn't need us; that sort of thing. It was just a piece of high land in my father's name. One of my father's friends introduced him to the wood business and told him that the mountain was a gold mine for him if he wanted to continue it. His friend took him to the mountains and introduced him to the people he had seen at work. With their assistance, my father established a woodworking business on the mountain. He formed an extremely friendly relationship with them. They, in turn, adored him. The business quickly grew and prospered. My father made a lot of money from the business. At the same time, he paid the men who worked for him very well. My father knew everything about them—where did they come from? What was their history? What was their way of life, culture, and ethical background? He had a long list of things he wanted to do for them. Unfortunately, my father was unable to grant his wishes. He died at a young age. I took over his business after he died. The men at work provided me with all of the assistance I required to run the business successfully. It was founded on mutual trust, gain, and a friendly relationship. To be honest, I don't know as much about them as my father did. They are settled on the other side of the mountain. They are a cheerful bunch who have kept my business afloat. They like me as much as I like them. I'm curious if they love me the way they used to love my father. I've remained mostly engrossed in the business as it has grown over time."

Ananth heard him with great interest. "After hearing you, I became more curious to know about the men at work and the wood business," Ananth said when his friend finished. He then continued, "As I said before, I am not from a business family and have no knowledge of how to conduct business. But, based on what I've seen, I'd love to stay with you for an extended period. It would be an exciting and rewarding experience for me. This experience, I suppose, will be beneficial to me before I decide about my career. I'm wondering if you could accommodate my wish in your overall business framework." His friend replied, "You are most welcome to join me in whatever way you like. Even your presence here would provide me with good company, which would boost my energy for work. At the same time, you will gain a better understanding of the woodworking industry. More importantly, you can mingle with the men at work who have piqued your interest. They will regard you as someone who has come here to supervise how the work is progressing. Don't hesitate to let me know if you want to go back to the plains. I'll make all of the necessary arrangements for you."

Ananth's journey began. Every morning, he accompanied his friend to his place of work. His friend used to visit different spots, while a group leader used to take him around different places to explain to him the work that was going on. In this way, one at a time he learned a lot of wood cutting art and business. When he got home in the evening, he would have a nice dinner with his friend, relax, and talk over any number of topics before retiring to bed. As time went on, Ananth became very friendly with the people at work. They began calling him Ana. They would share their meals with him, talk about their lives, take him near the fountain that flowed from the top of the hill, and tell him many interesting stories. From afar, his friend noticed his association with the people. He maintained silence about it.

During his daily routine, Ana noticed an interesting event taking place shortly after noon every day. In the middle of a low area stood a large banyan tree. A ring of smaller trees encircled the larger tree. Many of the tree's offshoot trunks penetrated the ground, it looked as if the tree were supported by a network of trunks. Just before noon, the air would be unusually calm. A silence would roll like oil in every corner. Suddenly, a few moments later, it would be broken by the rustling of the banyan tree's leaves. The wind would appear out of nowhere, as if it had been waiting for this moment. Other trees' branches would start swinging, creating a cacophony of rustling leaves and whizzing sounds through the tree's branches. The birds would start singing. Men at work would gather around the tree, bow down, and sing a song in their native tongue. The rustling of the leaves ceased; the wind cooled; the birds stopped singing; and the men returned to their work after a brief respite. When Ana saw it for the first time, it was a breath-taking scene. Later, he asked one of the men what it was all about and how such a strange thing could happen. "Since I grew up and started working here, I had witnessed it every day except when there was a snowfall," the man replied, "what I learned from the elders was that they had worshipped the wind as one of their gods for generations. They existed because the wind did. That's all there is to it. It had no faith attached to it. Faith was tied to the old banyan tree, through which the wind appeared as God to hear their prayers. The wind chose the old banyan tree because it was the oldest of all the trees here. Furthermore, the wind directed the old tree to look after them and care for their lively hood. So, they worshipped the old tree as well, and with its blessings, they continued their woodworking." Ana was moved by his straightforward explanation of what he witnessed with his own eyes. The man gradually became his close friend after that incident. He offered a name to the man—Krishi.

Every day, Ana and Krishi would go on a tour of the majority of the work sites, gossiping together. Krishi had a lot of stories to tell. He was relieved to have found a friend with whom he could share his stories. Ana, too, had a lot of questions. He found the answers to his questions from Krishi one by one. Ana once asked Krishi, "What other gods do you worship?" "The sun god, the moon god, the earth god, and the water god," Krishi replied. "Don't you have any other gods worshipped on special occasions?" Ana asked. "No. They are the only gods for us, and it is because of them that we survive," Krishi replied. It was a revelation for Ana. The gods he named were all well-known and were worshipped in various forms by many people. Aside from that, people worshiped a variety of other gods. In God's kingdom, there is no dearth of gods. Ana thought these people were a different breed, worshipping for a single reason: survival. They were inextricably linked with God for their very existence and they expressed their gratitude to Him through prayers. This concept piqued his interest, and he was eager to learn more about their worship.

Ana once inquired of Krishi, "How do you worship the water God?" "First, let me describe how we worship the sun god," Krishi replied, "Then I'll take you to the top of the mountain to tell you about and show how we worship the water god." Krishi began walking up the hills after saying this. Ana trailed after him. On the way, he began, "Every morning when the sun rises from behind the mountain tip on the eastern side, the women of the village get up. They hold a disc of the fine white net in their hands, pointing it at the sun. As the sky stooping over the hilltop turns red, so does the white net. The sun gradually ascends in the sky. Even on a cloudy or snowy day, they hold the disc in the same manner. The dense red cloud over the mountain peak paints the disc red. The birds fly around in circles in the sky. The women sing a chorus in praise of the sun god. The birds too join in on the chorus. Following that, they present the sun with some sweet and water. To begin the day, they take a glass of water as if both they and God need a glass of water to start the day's work."

For a long time, they walked in silence. All the while, Ana was trying to picture in his mind what Krishi had narrated to him. They finally made it to the top of the mountain. It was afternoon. The spring water glowed in the sunlight. Krishi knelt and drank some water from the fold of his palm. It's clean spring water here," he said as he turned toward Ana, "if you're thirsty, you might as well drink it." Ana sipped the water. It had a sweet taste. Krishi described how the stream flowed from higher up the other mountain range and snaked through a series of bents down to this point. They both began walking upstream. They came to a halt after about a half-kilometer walk. A spectacular scene unfolded in front of Ana. Two natural fountains bounced up from the spring. There were a few large boulders scattered throughout the area, as well as a few rocky outcrops. The entire formation of the terrain had thrust up the water like fountains. As the beams of sunlight penetrated the fountains, they shone brightly. The breeze was gentle, the stream flowing through the boulders was musical, and the dense forest on the other side of the stream formed a green shed. "We worship the two fountains as our water god," Krishi explained. "How do you do that? Do you come up here every day to offer your prayers?" Ana inquired. "No. None of us climb up to this point daily." Saying that he pointed to a small hut some distance away from the stream. They made their way over to the hut. Inside, there was an elderly man. He had longhairs and beards that were almost as long as his hairs. They were whitish-grey. "He is our priest," Krishi explained, "He worships the water god twice a day, once in the early morning and once when the sun sets, on behalf of the villagers. We take

149

care of the priest and his livelyhood. In the hut, he has all of the necessities. The senior member of his family has done this job for the entire village for generations. The people of the village have the highest regard for him and his family." Ana was only surprised at how he got protection from wild animals that might come near the stream in the middle of the night. When he enquired about it, Krishi replied innocently, "The water god is his protector."

After dinner that night, Ana told his friend about what he had learned from Krishi about the worship of the sun god and the water god. His friend quietly listened to Ana before remarking, "Though not in such detail, I was aware of their worship of various gods." What I witnessed was an elaborate display of their worship of the earth god. They invited me to their festival once. Their worship of the earth god was very similar to that of the plains people who did it in mid-April. Their festival would take place over three days. They wouldn't show up to work on those days. They made a variety of sweets and foods, distributed them among themselves, and visited each other's homes. The only difference I noticed in their festival was that they fed every cow in the village three times a day for three days. They believed that it was a part of the earth god who provided them with grains to eat and survive. Regularly, they bow down to the earth before beginning to plough the land.

Ana learned a lot about the woodworking business in a short period. But, more importantly, he got close and personal with the tribal people. Because of his carefree, simple, and lovable nature, they began to love him as if he were one of their own. In turn, he was willing to go to any length for them. This bond grew stronger over time as Ana learned more about their cultural and ethical backgrounds, as well as how they came to live in this location.

They came here from far off—generations before. They were only eighteen people when they first arrived at this location as migrants. They were poor dirt farmers with scant farm tools, clothing, cookware, and knives. They visited several locations, stayed for a while, and then left the place. The entourage continued their march in this manner, moving toward mountains and forests. The reasons why people preferred forests and mountains over plains were simply their preferences for the variety of nature. The women in the entourage were lovers and worshipers of nature in its most basic form. They truly loved to stay with the simple nature in the most simple way. When they got close to the mountains, they felt more connected to nature.

Presumably, they were the first settlers in this area. There was no record of when they settled here, how they grew over generations, and how they transformed into a unique tribe. Some survived in the form of stories passed down through generations, but the majority were likely to have vanished into obscurity as unrecorded history.

One day, while they were on their visit to work sites, Krishi unexpectedly told Ana, "You are going to stay tonight with me in our village." Ana stared at him on his face and asked, "Is there anything special tonight?" Krishi responded quickly, tonight is the full moon night and I'd like to show you how we worship the moon god. Aside from that, you might have a wonderful night that you have never had before. When Ana accompanied them to their village in the evening, everyone at work was overjoyed.

They arrived at the village's outskirts as the sun set behind the hills. The sky above the hilltop was tinged with red. A few brushstroke clouds in the sky edging the hills also turned red as they moved lazily over the mountains. On the other side, a full moon was visible in the sky. It was far behind the center of the sky and was still dressed in yellow. They ambled down the hilly path for a while before arriving at a plateau. The majority of the houses were built on the plateau, which extended for a long distance before descending as a mountain slope. The houses were separated by trees. Krishi led Ana inside a house after they arrived in the village. Two nice beds were resting on the two sides of a large room. It was a mud house, but it was polished and colored on the inside. On two opposite walls, there were two small windows. Krishi asked him to change into one of their traditional dresses and rest. Meanwhile, a girl brought two earthen pots of hot tea and some snacks. "Take rest before I wake you up," Krishi said as he accompanied him to the so-called evening tea, "Today you're going to have a long night."

Ana had fallen into a deep sleep. In the midst of it, he dreamed of a cow standing beneath a tree with two bells attached to its two horns, inquiring about him. One of the villagers asked why it desired to know about him. It responded, "Tonight, I want to dance with him in front of everyone else. I'll take him with me after the dance to the top of that small hillock where he could touch the feet of the moon god, who would bless him with the marriage of his choice to the best-looking girl in the village." Ana's sweet dream was shattered by a few strokes on his back. He found Krishi standing in front of him and saying, "Change your clothes and get ready for the festival night." Ana noticed Krishi wearing a brightly colored dress and brought for him a similar outfit.

When Ana stepped out of the door, he was surprised to see a different village than the one he had seen earlier in the evening. A startling white full moon had shown up in the sky. The village was illuminated by hundreds of neon lights as it were. Everything around him was gleaming white. Krishi took him to the center of

152

the village, where there was a large open space. Everyone in the village had gathered there, dressed brightly. The women had flower crowns in their hair. The air was filled with a chorus of lough and humming. A large copper plate half filled with water was laid in the center of the ground. Ana had never seen a plate of that size before. The white moon along with a portion of the sky and a few light white patches of cloud, peered into the plate.

Men and women flocked around Ana as he arrived at the venue. He was greeted with a grand welcome with a variety of joyful sounds. A young woman approached him, took his hand in hers, and led him around the large plate. "We shall worship the moon god, while keeping the plate in the center," she said with a smile, "all of the men and women, including you, will dance around the plate." She pointed to a few people standing with musical instruments, and said, "Those are the people who will provide the accompanying music. In this way, we worship the moon god once a month. We eat and drink after offering the food to god during our dance and music." Ana listened to her with a smile on his face and then said, "I am no expert in dancing or drinking." But I'd be delighted to join you." "Don't worry," the girl said spontaneously, "I'll dance with you, make you dance, sing, and drink with me. You'd be an expert dancer by the time the event is over." "Are you a dance teacher?" Ana inquired. She responded with a smile through the corner of her eyes. "I need to learn to dance because I have to dance with someone else tonight," Ana said. "Who?" Inquired the young lady. "I'll break the suspense another time," Ana replied.

The event began. An elderly man shattered three coconuts and poured water onto the plate. Flowers were strung around the plate like a necklace. Several bowls containing various sweets surrounded it. The elderly man then bowed in front of the plate, stood up, and began dancing. The sounds of an orchestra were afloat in the air produced by the drums, conches, and windpipes, which were swallowed by the expanse of the nearby dense forest on the hills. Everyone began dancing to the beat of the music. Ana was set in motion by the young lady, who began dancing with him. Ana discovered he was dancing with someone else a few moments later. The lady had vanished amid the crowd. He attempted to locate Krishi. He, too, was lost in the crowd. Even though Ana was dancing slowly, it seemed to him, as if, everything around him was in a rhythmic motion. There was no difference between men and women. Everyone was transformed into particles of black dots that moved in pulses. Who was dancing with whom was no longer in anyone's control; it was driven by the current of the motion. Ana couldn't remember when he began eating and drinking with others and joining their chorus of songs. The young lady did appear out of nowhere at times, drink and dance with him, and then vanished.

Suddenly, Ana felt that the moonlight had washed away everything around him. It was only the moonlight's whiteness that existed. He wasn't even able to feel his own body. He couldn't make out anything in the distance. He had been reduced to a mere concept. He was floating in space. He was drifting in a void, somewhere across the line dividing a delightful glow and reality. He remained in that state of being until he felt a soft gentle touch carry him away to some distant location and rested him somewhere. Then, a complete blankness engulfed him.

When he awoke, he found himself on the bed. The other bed was vacant. Krishi had gotten up and left, or he might not have slept there at all. He was attempting to guess the time, which could be anything because there was only a dim light coming in through the two small windows. He looked up and tried to recall the previous night. Various events flashed through his mind. Suddenly, the door to the room opened, and in walked Krishi, who was followed by the young lady holding a plate in her hand. "It's only noon," Krishi said as he walked in. "I figured I'd wake you up for breakfast even if you weren't awake." The lady placed the plate on the floor, neatly arranging three earthen pots of hot tea alongside a variety of snacks. Krishi and the lady both took a seat on the floor. Ana got out of bed, washed, and joined them. While sipping her tea, the lady burst out laughing and described everything Ana did last night. "Everyone loved your presence at the function," she said, "they liked how you drank with them, danced with them, and sang with them. Many ladies hugged you, kissed you on the cheek, and danced with their arms around your waist." "I could vaguely recall some of them," Ana replied, "did you dance with me and kiss me like that?" "Of course, I did," the lady replied, "I was the first to begin it. You might not remember them because you were high. Toward the end of the function, me and Krishi brought you to the room and laid you on the bed." Ana laughed aloud and said, "Thank you for everything you did. I must say that I thoroughly enjoyed last night's events. I wish I was in my senses when you kissed my cheek and danced with your arms around me. Then I would have planted a kiss on your cheek as well." "You certainly missed out on the opportunity to experience them through your senses. But you could kiss my cheeks right now. At least, you'd get a taste of what all you could not taste." She moved closer to Ana after saying that. Ana kissed her on the cheek. Krishi was ecstatic and held Ana in his arms.

"I don't think you need to go to work today," Krishi said, "you could take a bath, eat lunch, and walk around the village. Junaki will show you all the sights before taking you up the hill and putting you in the right spot where I will meet you. She is familiar with all of the locations here, as well as many other things. You might come across them while taking a round with her." "Why didn't you tell her name at the outset?" Ana retorted, "It's a lovely name." They all laughed together.

Junaki and Ana set out after lunch to explore the village. What surprised Ana was that each of the houses had one or more paintings on its walls. It was a portrait of a few dancing women in one, men beating drums in the other, and a few deer or other animals grazing on the field in another. There wasn't a single house that didn't have a painting. The path winded through the trees, taking numerous detours to various destinations. Each house's surroundings were neatly laid out with a good layer of soil. "Is everyone here a painter?" Ana inquired of Junaki. "No. In the village, not everyone is a painter. If that's the case, who earned the food and shelter? The majority of the painters are village women. Again, not all ladies enjoy painting. A few of them are drawn to this art. "I collaborate with them to make the entire village look colorful," Junaki explained. "I see what Krishi was implying now. You are the village's chief painter. You must be teaching young girls and women to paint. That is both amazing and wonderful. When I first looked into your eyes, my intuition told me you were unique. "My senses did not deceive me," Ana said. "But your senses were playing tricks on you last night," she chuckled.

"I know a little bit about painting, but only on canvas. We are used to painting with oil colors. However, I noticed that the colors used in the paintings here are not the same as those used in the oil paintings. They are not also watercolor. Moreover, I can't imagine painting on neat earth layers as a canvas. It's quite fascinating to me," Ana said. Junaki began, "It appears you know a lot about painting. Yes, you are entirely correct. The colors are

156

neither entirely oil nor entirely water-based. We prepare the colors ourselves using various flowers, leaves, and fruit juices. We add mustard extracts, which provide a kind of oil base to it. Painting on a soil canvas differs from painting on a conventional canvas. To begin, a light charcoal outline of a figure is drawn on the wall. The area within the figure is then covered with thick brush strokes of a base color. It's left to dry for two days. During this time, the soil absorbs a significant amount of color, leaving a firm-colored base on which the actual painting is done. You could call it a colored canvas. For painting, we use a variety of brushes made of jute or other fibres." Ana stared her in the face the entire time she was explaining. He discovered a different Junaki, an artist with oratory eloquence and a passionate glow on her face.

"I'd love to learn how to paint on mud walls. I don't mind becoming your student. I'm sure I'll make time in my work schedule to practice painting on the walls. I hope you don't have any objections to what I'm proposing," Ana said. Junaki first smiled at him, then burst out laughing pouring in musical sounds of mountain spring. "You are most welcome to learn painting here." she exclaimed. "Perhaps by looking at you, many others will be inspired to learn this art. Let's go up the hills before the sun sets. The sun has already stooped to low in the sky. I have to get you to Krishi on time." Both started walking up the hills, leaving the village on the plateau behind. Junaki climbed at a much faster rate than Ana. He was following her. Junaki had to lend Ana her hands at times to assist him to climb faster.

They arrived at the designated location on time. Krishi was there to greet them. "How was your day with Junaki?" he inquired of Ana. Ana responded quickly, "I had a great time with her. Moreover, many intriguing aspects of Junaki were revealed

157

during the trip. You had chosen an all-rounder to be my guide. Thank you very much." "May more opportunities to explore her fully come your way? Let me now take you to your friend who is waiting for you to return home. We shall return to our village once I hand you over to your friend," said Krishi.

Ana and his friend arrived home in time. They ate dinner together and relaxed with cups of coffee after dinner, as they did every day. "How was your trip to the village?" his friend inquired of Ana. Ana began to describe every detail of his visit to his friend. His friend locked his gaze on him and listened intently to everything he said. "I didn't know you had the skill of painting," his friend retorted after he finished, "my father was an avid painter who produced a large number of works himself. He had no intention of becoming a businessman. He started the woodworking business at the insistence of a friend. Most likely, my father was drawn to this tribe of people after learning that the women of the village had this artistic flair. Inwardly, he may have begun to appreciate their simplicity, culture, and artistic sense. He began to adore them. They, in turn, adored him. That's how he developed a close relationship with this group of people. He had a lot of ideas for their well-being. If you want to help them, I will always be there for you. You don't have to be too involved in the woodworking industry. Your company would be sufficient for me to move the company forward." Ana replied, "I haven't given it much thought yet. Please allow me some time. I'll get back to you as soon as I have a concrete idea."

A few uneventful days passed by. Both of them used to come to the work site in time. Ana would accompany Krishi to various sites. They would return to the banyan tree just at noon to worship the wind god. After that, they shared lunch and went on another site-seeing excursion. They didn't have much discussion about

Ana's trip to the village. Once and only once Krishi said, "Junaki was asking how you were doing, and if she had displayed any inappropriate behavior, she should be excused for it." "She is a gem of a woman," Ana replied, laughing, "I'd never met such a talented and lovely lady before. Her features are appropriate for a beauty queen contest. She can win the contest with a little colored make-up." "I shall tell her everything you have said about her. Her joys would be limitless," Krishi exclaimed. Ana replied, "Don't tell her anything about all of this. I have some ideas for your village. I'll meet her and her people in the village once it's crystallized. Keep it to yourself until then."

Time flew by. On one inconspicuous evening, after dinner, when the two friends talked about a variety of topics over cups of coffee, Ana began, "I have made a few plans for the village that I need to discuss with you. I'll get started as soon as you approve them." His friend was eager to hear. "First and foremost, I would teach myself the art of painting on the mud wall," he continued, "that would be the beginning. I am confident that, as Junaki predicted, many women and children will step forward to learn the art. I plan to open a few art galleries in the village gradually. People from within and outside the village would be welcome to paint in the galleries. I want to color every piece of rock that has protruded from the village's surroundings!"

He continued, "My next goal would be to establish a primary school in the village. I wish that every young boy and girl in the village received a basic education. If the ladies of the village so desire, they may join the school. The third thing I'd like to establish is a primary health care unit. The community as a whole is in excellent health. They are not typically disease prey. Their small ailments are usually treated with herbal medicine, in which the majority of the village people are well versed. That unit should only be used in an emergency. Finally, I would like to establish a conference hall where people can gather on occasion to discuss general issues concerning the village welfare. They do it now as well. However, they don't have a forum."

"You don't have to ask for my approval for what you've planned to do," his friend said after carefully listening to him, "as I previously stated, I am always on your side with whatever plan you devise for the village. It's not just you doing it for the benefit of the village. I'm silently present there. Don't hesitate to ask for assistance whenever you need it. You, Krishi, and Junaki plan out every detail. You don't need to devote much time to the wood business. You divide your time between village work and woodwork in your unique way. As for the money, just tell me how much you want and I'll make it available to you." "Thank you for your wholehearted support and silent presence with us for the project," Ana said, "in a day or two, I'll convene a meeting of the entire village to discuss our strategy. Of course, I'll have a meeting with Krishi and Junaki first."

Ana had a quick meeting with Krishi and Junaki the next day. They were both overjoyed to listen to his proposals. They suggested Ana speak with the villagers on Sunday when everyone would be at home. On Saturday night, Ana, Krishi, and Junaki had a fun dinner together. They danced as a group of three, with Junaki in the center. It was a simple folk dance. Ana could easily keep up with the dance's rhythmic steps. Junaki chuckled, "Soon you'd be the village's dance master." "Provided you dance with me now with some difficult rhythmic steps for which you must catch hold of me teach," Ana replied. Ana and Junaki began dancing in a different rhythm, with Junaki assisting Ana to perform. While they were dancing, Krishi burst out laughing.

The next morning, the villagers gathered in the village

center. The village's oldest man announced that Ana would like to speak to all of the villagers. Ana spoke to them in simple terms about his plans and the motivations behind them. After Ana finished, everyone began to dance joyfully. Many of them rushed up to Ana and embraced him. The oldest man then stood up and declared that Ana would be in charge of all village decisions from now on. He gladly delegated this task to Ana. Ana immediately reacted, "The chief of the village would continue to be the senior most man. Whatever action we take, we will do so with his permission and blessing." The old man embraced Ana. Tears of emotion rolled down his cheeks.

The project got underway. With Junaki's help, Ana began painting on the mud walls. Many children and young ladies showed up to begin learning the art. Soon, there was almost no place in the village that was left unpainted. Junaki was astounded to see Ana painting so delicately on the mud walls. She told Ana that he must have been painting regularly before. Ana responded, "Association is most important when painting. How could he create a mediocre painting in front of her?" They built three long mud walls to keep the spirit of painting in motion. They erected sheds over them with a few patches of openings to allow light to pass through. The location of the painting gradually shifted to the walls, which eventually became a gallery.

Ana's next project began. He built a school on the outskirts of the village with the help of the villagers. It was a large, well-lit, and airy hall. There were no benches or chairs. Everyone would take their seats on the floor. He arranged for a large blackboard from the plains as well as dozens of school books. His friend readily made them available to him. The children were taught in the morning and then released at twelve noon to help their family members in the fields. Junaki took the initiative to start the women's school for two hours in the afternoon. It was difficult to get off to a good start at first. However, many of the village's women soon came forward. Ana, Krishi, and two young men who had stayed in the plains for a while ran the school. Ana, Krishi, and Junaki were overjoyed to see that their efforts had paid off.

Meanwhile, Ana's friend sent a young man to the plains, where he was able to place the young man in a small hospital with the help of hisfriend. He learned the majority of the nurses work there. He also learned the names of some medications that can be used safely. Within a year, he returned to the village and established a small healthcare emergency unit.

Ana's final project was to complete the village hall, where villagers would meet and discuss various village issues. Ana anticipated that it would be more of a gathering place for gossiping, as the villagers had a few serious issues to discuss. They were a happy and peaceful group of people. They had plenty of land for farming. Everyone had a comfortable place to stay. Nobody could ever imagine going hungry in the village because there was so much food. Most importantly, everyone was eager to assist one another in the event of a problem. On one side of the village, a nice village hall was built. The villagers worked together to give it the best appearance possible; it was a large circular hall with the best painters in the village painting both the inside and outside of the hall. From the inside, it appeared to be more of a painting gallery. It took nearly two years of collaboration with villagers to give Ana's vision a physical form. During this time, he lived in the village on occasions and with his friend on others.

In one after-dinner session, Ana spent a long time with his friend after the projects were finished. "I could never have imagined I'd be able to complete my task so quickly," he began, "the villagers were so cooperative, hardworking, and enthusiastic that I was able to finish my mission. To be honest, they treated it as their own. They poured their hearts and souls into it. The sincerity, love, friendliness, and honesty of the women in the village astounded me. They are, indeed, a different breed of people. I wish our tiny planet was teeming with such people. It would have been a very different world."

His friend was staring at him the entire time he was speaking. His friend retorted after he finished, "I knew you'd be successful in your endeavor in a short period. I noticed you and Krishi working for the village from a distance. What I gathered from the villagers at work was that they regard you as one of their own. They want you to stay with them permanently. That is something I wish you could do. As for me, they began to regard me as their Godfather, which was the furthest thing from my mind. What you've accomplished thus far is unfathomable. I only have one small question. That is related to their education. Why didn't you want to expand the school beyond the primary level?"

"To be honest, it was by design," Ana replied, "I didn't want them to go to the plains for higher education. I wished for them to remain in their village and preserve their culture and identity. To be more specific, I wanted them to stay connected to nature as they are. They will be uprooted from their own culture once they begin to live in the plains for an extended period. Their beauty, which is hidden in their simplicity, honesty, and concern for one another would be lost. More importantly, they would forget to earn a living by putting in hard work. They don't have to look for work as long as they stay farmers. After all, farming is not a bad profession. I don't believe in education that takes away your simplicity and purity of heart providing job opportunities only. They don't need any additional education as long as they have good hygiene, discipline, and a well-organized work environment. What difference would it make if they discovered that the moon is not God, but rather a planet that revolves around the Earth? When you and I look at the moon, we rarely consider it to be revolving around our globe. Rather, we marvel at the sight of a startling half or quarter moon set in a sky."

"Perhaps you have a point in what you say," his friend said after carefully listening to him, "I mentioned it because the general public's perception of education is strongly linked to the profession. These people don't have a scarcity of food or shelter as long as they are willing to work hard. I believe they are a joyful group of a good human beings."

Ana's life revolved around the village and the woodwork up in the hills. He continued to stay with his friend at times and in the village at others. One day, on his way back from school with Junaki, she asked him about the dance he was supposed to do with someone on that eventful night of moon God worship. "Do you remember what I said so long ago?" Ana replied. Junaki responded, "I remember everything I come across, especially with you." Ana then told her about his dream and what the cow said to him. Junaki laughed for a long while before saying, "Indeed, there is a hilltop from which you get the feeling that you have touched the feet of the moon god once you extend your hand toward the moon—that's the villagers' belief." "Did you try it yourself?" Ana inquired. "No," Junaki replied, "I might accompany you if you are interested." Ana readily agreed to participate in the adventure. Junaki suggested that they would try it out one day before the full moon because she couldn't leave the village on the night of the moon god's worship.

Ana and Junaki began their ascent of the hill the day before a full moon. The sky was appallingly clear and utterly cloudless. The nearly full moon appeared in the sky as a white disk. The moonlight cast a bright light on the hill, village, and forest trees. Everything appeared to be crystal clear. They had no trouble getting to the top. Junaki was ahead of Ana and helped him up some stretches of the hill from time to time. After about a half-hour climb, they came across a small stream. They sat beside the stream, splashing water on their faces. Junaki drank the water from her hand's fold. Ana imitated her. The breeze was gentle, and the stream's water sparkled in the moonlight. The night birds cooed softly. "I don't like leaving the place," Ana said. Junaki responded, "The moon god cannot wait for us all night. Furthermore, there are animals here who would enjoy a nice feast tonight if we stayed a little longer." Suddenly, there was a cry of a big bird, a cry which Ana had never heard before. The cry reverberated in the space. The silence returned to every corner after the bird had flown away. They stood up and began climbing again. They arrived at the top of the hill after another fifteen minutes of climbing. The top of the hill was unobstructed. The rocks protruded from the ground, forming a small plateau. Ana looked around from the top of the hill. Everything from there looked splendid in the moonlight night. He cast a glance down at the village in the distance. It appeared to be a miniature painting on a green canvas. Junaki asked Ana to look up, adore the moon god, and close his eyes. Ana pleaded with junaki to follow what he was doing. Junaki replied, "Of course, I shall also touch the feet of the moon god. I have traveled up here with you. How could I go back without having the blessings of the moon god?" Both closed their eyes and stretched their hands up toward the sky. Suddenly Ana felt that he had entered a fairyland.

165

Everything was white there. The night angels were flying in space. The air was filled with the scent of some unknown flowers. The night birds were singing. Ana had no sooner tried to feel the moon god's feet than he heard a whisper in his ears, "She is yours. Take care of her and live a happy life." Ana opened his eyes to find himself locked with Junaki, her head resting on his shoulder. He heard a faint ringing of a bell. He looked forward. The cow was standing a little further away from him, staring at them. Its horns were adorned with two bells. Ana patted Junaki on the back and exclaimed, "Look!" "What?" Junaki inquired. By then, the cow had vanished.

The next morning, Krishi arrived with Junaki to meet Ana for breakfast. They all sat on the floor and shared breakfast. Ana had just finished his last sip of tea when he announced his intention to marry Junaki. Krishi leaped to his feet, began dancing, and then embraced Ana in joy. Junaki couldn't stop laughing the entire time. The news quickly spread throughout the village. Many villagers rushed to congratulate Ana and Junaki. They were married on the next full moon day. Because it was also the day for the moon god worship, the marriage turned into a big festival. The entire night was spent having fun. Only after the sun worship could the couple go for a rest. Ana's friend joined everyone else in the village and didn't return until the night was done.

Ana and Junaki's lives began to change. They had been friends for a long time. They now had to make a home together. They both worked hard to build a lovely home for themselves. The villagers banded together to make their dream a reality. Ana's schedule became busier than ever. He had to manage both the school and the woodworking business. Junaki assumed sole responsibility for preserving the spirit of painting among the village's ladies. Ana made it a point to keep his friend entertained on occasion. They would eat dinner together and talk about whatever they wanted during the relaxing period after dinner.

On one such occasion, Ana was informed by his friend that a painter from abroad had expressed an interest in visiting the village after learning everything there was to know about it. His friend had himself told the painter the story of the village. His friend requested Ana to take him around the village and show him all of the artwork. Ana agreed with pleasure.

The painter was an elderly man who made a fortune through his art. As Ana took him around the village, he was astounded by the paintings on the walls. He'd never tried painting on a mud wall before. It was a revelation for him. He was transfixed by the artwork on the walls. He couldn't believe it when he discovered that the majority of the painters were village women. It had never occurred to him that so-called tribal women could be such talented painters. He realized that painters are not bound by race, creed, color, or gender.

Instead of spending two to three days in the village, he spent a fortnight there, not only admiring every painting in the village but also learning the art of painting on the walls. Junaki had given him the company all along. Only after witnessing the charming moon god worship, he left the village. Before leaving, he promised Junaki that he would come to the village off and on, and project the village to the outside world.

The village quickly became a hub for painters. Painters from all over began to visit the village. They would stay in the village for a few days, learn how to paint on the mud wall, and then display their creations in the mud wall gallery. Ana had to build several small huts in the village to house the painters. They enjoyed their stay in the village as well as the simple food served to them. They also enjoyed touring and trekking to various hilly locations. The villagers' simple and lovable nature impressed them the most. Another thing they admired was the villagers' hygiene and cleanliness. They couldn't believe the tribal people could keep their environment so clean. With the little English they learned in school, the schoolchildren assisted in establishing communication between the visitors and the village people.

Ana made it clear that the village would provide free hospitality to visitors as long as they stayed in the village. However, the visitors insisted on paying the villagers for the services they provided. Finally, an agreement was reached in which the visitors would contribute to the village welfare fund, which would be used to improve the village's prosperity. Ana used that money to build a few more painting galleries, expand the school, build a good children's library, and build a sports complex for the kids.

Within a short period, the village became well known as a painter's village. Ana's friend built a nice guesthouse in a beautiful mountain location for the convenience of visitors. He entrusted Ana with the care of the village's visitors.

All of the village's events occurred within five years of Ana's arrival on the mountain. One day, his friend unexpectedly asked Ana to spend the evening with him. The two friends had a nice dinner together and then relaxed over cups of coffee, as they had done previously. While sipping his coffee, his friend informed Ana that his father died exactly ten years hence.

Before his death, his father informed him that a piece of paper had been preserved in a small chest for him to read after ten years. His friend had never touched the chest for so long. "I am going to open the chest on this very momentous day after ten years of my father's death," his friend told Ana, "and I'd like to do it in front of you. I needed your help to get it done." His friend walked up to a shelf and rested his hand on a small chest. He opened the chest and took out a small piece of paper from it. It had almost turned yellow. His friend returned to his seat near him, unfolded the paper, and began reading.

"My son, when you read this note, someone will be sitting next to you to listen to what you are reading." After reading this far, his friend offered a long look at him and continued, "You know, I loved the village folk a lot. As a painter myself, I was impressed by their talent. I had a lot of plans for the welfare of those villagers. I am sorry for not being able to meet them. But I knew that someone will come here and finish my task someday. Wait until that time. When you read this note, the person who will make my dream come true will be sitting next to you. Please offer my heartfelt gratitude and blessings to him."

Ana cast a glance out the window. A stunning white moon appeared in the sky. Light white clouds had gathered on one side of the moon. They all took on the form of a human being and began moving over the moon, blanketing it. The figure glistened in the moonlight. "Look!" Exclaimed Ana as he stroked his friend. His friend yelled, "Daad!" as he looked out the window. The figure gradually disintegrated as it crossed the moon.

Valley of Silence

"Are you familiar with the Valley of Silence?" my friend inquired. I responded, "Of course, yes. I've also heard a lot of stories about it. They appeared to me as fairy tales replete with mystic encounters. According to what I had heard, those who touched the valley vanished instantly. After a long period of oblivion, only a few monks who had been there could return." My friend retorted that he, too, had heard stories about the valley similar to mine. The stories, according to him, could have come from the monks who had returned; otherwise, there would have been no story; a person who had vanished couldn't tell a story. He also stated that the overall theme piqued his interest in visiting the location and asked if I wanted to accompany him. "Give me some time to think about it," I said, "Meanwhile, you could learn more about its exact location and how to get there. You could also get more information about its history from the people who live nearby."

We met again a few days later. My friend gathered a lot more information about the valley and its history by that point. As we began talking, he said, "The valley of silence is surrounded by Himalayan mountains and is uninhabited by any living creature. It is located on the Tibetan border and is always covered with snow. At any time of day, the entire valley looks spectacular. The valley and its surroundings turn red in the early morning when the sun rises. The color slowly changes to shades of red before finally becoming gleaming white with the sun atop the sky. As the sun sets, the shadows cast by the surrounding mountains on the valley turn gradually into black, covering everything in a dark blanket. The valley stands quiet, with only particles of silence moving from one corner to the other. The nearest habitat is one hundred kilometers away, in a settlement inhabited by a hilly tribe. The tribe primarily adheres to a form of Buddhist culture. Whoever traveled to the valley had to go through this settlement. All stories about the valley have emanated from the people of the settlement."

I asked, "What is the common perception of the people about the valley?" My friend answered, "The people's general perceptions about the valley are tinted with magical experiences. The valley is generally thought to be haunted. The belief is, departed souls inhabit it. Whoever enters the valley never returns. Many people claim to have witnessed people vanish once they entered the valley. However, another group believes that aliens from another planet have settled there. They cannot be seen with the naked eye because they have a different state of existence. Humans who enter the valley are instantly transformed into aliens and begin to live like them. This group believed what monks said about the valley spending a period of stay with the aliens." "How could they return if annihilated by the valley's atmosphere?" I wondered. "By the spiritual power, they attained," my friend replied.

I said, "It's one thing to be intrigued; it's quite another to act on it. Regardless of the various fantasies that might tempt us to visit the location, there is an element of risk lurking in the background. We don't know what the truth is. Is it prudent to accept complete uncertainty to discover the truth?" "It appears you have some reservations about embarking on an adventure," my friend said after carefully listening to me, "You won't be able to move forward unless you take it as an adventure. As for me, I'm intrigued by the overall theme, as I previously stated, and would like to go for the exploration. Uncertainty is a part of any adventure. Explorers invariably count death, the most unfavorable element, as one of the uncertainties. In this adventure, the worst is that we do not return from the Valley of Silence. We become silent forever."

"I agree with what you said," I told my friend, "And I'm just as excited to visit the location as you are. But I'd like to take a more cautious approach. If there are uncertainties, they should be minimum. Even so, the worst one would still be there. What I would recommend is that you include in your adventure a visit to one of the Buddhist monasteries in the valley's vicinity, such as a monastery near the Tibetan border. I am confident that within a two hundred kilometer radius of the location, there would be a few Tibetan monasteries. If the monks visited the site, they were possibly from those monasteries. More than that, if there is a mystery shrouding the valley of silence, the monks would undoubtedly be aware of it. Although I do not know spiritual powers assisting humans in encountering alien environments, our genes support such possibilities due to our heritage. Why not learn more about it from people who live and work on the subject?"

"There is something to what you said," my friend said, "It would be prudent to visit a monastery in the region before we visit the site. We can reach our destination by choosing a suitable route to provide us with all useful information."

We both agreed on the strategy. We set out for our mission on an inconspicuous day, not thinking about anything else. We had no strings attached to us. Both of our parents had left for heaven a long time ago. We were free birds to move around because we were the youngest people in our families and had the advantage of not having to look after anyone. Before we left, we said our goodbyes to the places where we had stayed so long. It was a finale, as it were, in case we didn't return.

We took a pre-planned route to the Tibetan border, close to the Valley of Silence. Once we got to the edge, we could figure out the nearest region with many Buddhist monasteries. It wasn't difficult for us to find it from the locals. We couldn't decide which monastery to visit when we arrived there. A monk came to our assistance. From him, we could gather that the largest monastery was only a kilometer away and had reasonable visitor accommodations. It also served as a center for teaching Buddhist practices and providing Buddhist courses. We finally arrived at the monastery.

The monastery stood in a lovely setting. No other monasteries were around. The sun rose from behind the Himalayan mountain range on the eastern side in the morning, traveled across the sky to its zenith, stooped down, and finally set behind the mountains on the western side. During its journey, it shed various colors over the monastery, setting every person within the monastery in motion to act in a specific way. The monks focused on prayers and meditation, while visitors were primarily interested in spiritual lectures, Buddhist yogic arts, and learning different types of prayers. A few visitors preferred to remain spectators.

We preferred to remain observers for two days before mingling with the monks. Our goal was to obtain as much information about the Valley of Silence and its mystic power as possible. We became close friends with two monks who provided comprehensive knowledge about the Buddhist way of life. We knew little about Buddhism, so we had no trouble understanding what they were saying. We also had a lengthy conversation with them about the various types of meditation practiced by Buddhist monks in different regions and countries. What we gathered was quite a revelation to us. According to them, whatever the style, the ultimate goal of all meditation practices was to achieve liberation, a state akin to cosmic nothingness that was difficult to describe. Meditation, they believed, empowered one with a high level of concentration and willpower. It was entirely up to the individual how he used that power. Usually, monks used that power to elevate their mental states to higher planes of existence, eventually attaining Nirvana. The higher their states of existence, the more peaceful and happy their minds became.

Many people used this power to develop many martial arts and fighting techniques. The fan fighting depicted in movies was an exaggerated version of those abilities. We learned from them that all masters of those arts and fighting abilities eventually diverted their attention and power to attain liberation toward the end of their lives.

We once asked them if spiritual power could ward off evil spirits or an alien environment. The monks were surprised at our inquiry. "We heard a valley of silence in the neighboring Himalayas where ghosts or aliens inhabit; they transform humans into their species. The majority of visitors never returned from the valley after they visited it. They had vanished. According to legend, only a few monks who had traveled to the location were able to return due to the spiritual power they had gained. The stories piqued our interest, wondering if something like this could happen," we stated.

A silence hovered between us for a while. Then the monks spoke, "We also have heard similar stories about the place but never bothered about it. True, some monks from other monasteries had visited the site. That happened a long time ago. We have no idea who they were or when they saw the place.

Furthermore, we have no idea how they managed to return from the valley. The most senior monk of our monastery might be aware of all you are eager to know. We might introduce you to him. He is an enlightened monk with whom you would enjoy conversing."

After two days, they introduced us to the senior monk. The monk didn't appear to be very old. However, we later learned that he was nearly ninety. With a lovely smile, he greeted us. In turn, we knelt before him to pay our respects. During our conversation, we became extremely friendly and wholly opened ourselves up to him, including our fears about visiting the Valley of Silence. After we finished, he began, "It is true that a few monks returned after visiting the site. However, it took them three years to return. I had lengthy discussions about their experiences with those monks. They appeared to be fantasies, but I believed them because monks told them. Stories are certainly enticing, and one would like to experience them. However, they are not worth putting one's life in danger to do so. I would not have done so for one simple reason: you can have a factually similar experience here, albeit not in the same way. The monks who had returned also realized the same thing later. I recommend that you consider becoming a monk in this monastery, acquire some spiritual experience, and then go on the adventure if you so desire. Then you wouldn't have to deal with the dilemma of obtaining the spiritual power required to come out of the alien environment."

"Certainly, we will consider your suggestion and get back to you as soon as we have some ideas," we said, "However, we would like to state unequivocally that the adventure is more appealing to us right now than becoming a monk. It doesn't matter if we stay here forever as monks or vanish into oblivion in the alien world, having nearly identical experiences to what we might have here." "Perhaps you could take a few days to go over our discussions and talk about it again," the monk suggested.

We returned with a half-full mind. Our concern went unanswered. We deliberated on our intention to visit the monastery for two days. We didn't come to the monastery to become monks, for sure. It was the farthest thing from our minds. However, the senior monk placed us in an unprecedented situation. Our meeting with the monks was eye-opening, and we received answers to many of our questions. Simultaneously, it was clear that legends about the Valley of Silence were not unfounded. That made us more willing to embark on the adventure. At the same time, undue anxiety lurked in the mind's background. We had only two options: either be lost in the world of aliens or be confined to the monastery as monks, as we didn't have to go back home. Both offered the possibility of experiencing a similar state of being, according to the senior monk. "What should we do?" we wondered.

We met the senior monk the next day, still undecided. He greeted us with the same warm smile. In exchange, we paid him our respects as before. "You're wondering what path you should take," he interrupted before we could begin, "Furthermore, many questions had gone unanswered in your mind. They had combined to perplex you. Confusion is the mind's worst enemy. So, it would help if you eliminated the confusion in the first place. Allow me to assist you in getting out of it." Saying this, he took out several bids threaded together in the form of a garland and said, "We chant some sacred sound while moving our fingers

176

over the bids. The chanting directs the mind inward. Following that, we meditate on our inner selves. These two are central to our spiritual practices. They are, however, aided by a few more ancillary practices, such as reading Buddhist scriptures. Typically, it takes a monk five to six years to become attuned to this practice. The spiritual journey then begins. Someone may achieve good spiritual power in four to five years, while others may require a little more time. The power gained is primarily used to draw the mind inward and attain firm determination. That was the only way the monks could leave the valley. They vowed before entering the valley that they would return, and they did."

We stood there silently and remorsefully, looking at the monk. We knew we'd never make it if this were the only way to gain the spiritual power needed to return from the alien world. "The spiritual power you described cannot be acquired as easily as we learned from you," we told the monk. "The adventure would lose its appeal by the time we achieve it. Like we said before, the adventure is more appealing to us right now than becoming monks here. Perhaps we will visit the location with the foreknowledge that we will never return."

The monk smiled at us and retorted, "I am glad both of you had been extremely candid with me. Speaking frankly does not imply speaking truthfully. The truth is revealed at the end; as you stated, you wish to visit the location even if you are not armed with any spiritual power. However, there was an undercurrent of sadness in your statement. You would have been pleased if I could have assisted you somehow. It was a silent wish. How could a monk let you leave empty-handed if you had silently or otherwise desired something from him? I pray Lord Buddha to protect you." We bowed reverently to his feet as a sign of our appreciation.

The following day, we set out for our destination. We purchased snow boots and jackets in preparation for the expected extreme cold weather in the valley. We passed through the hilly tribe's settlement and spoke with many people there. They were taken aback when they learned we were on our way to the valley. They vehemently opposed our plan, and they all told us the same stories we had already heard. Finally, knowing how determined we were to go, they gave us an excellent map to get there. The root was about hundred kilometers long. They recommended that we spend the nights on our way in small huts where some locals stay.

We arrived in the valley at noon on the fourth day. We were on top of a hill that surrounded the valley. It was blanketed in snow. So were the inner sides of the mountain, which merged with the plateau below. The valley was gleaming white in the midday sun. Silence rolled into every corner. It was such a quiet place that we could even hear our breathing. We stood there silently for a long time, not looking into the valley, not looking at the white slopes of the hill, not looking at the far-off peaks of the mountain; maybe we were staring at nothing.

My friend broke the silence, "Let's have the last lunch on this planet. According to all legends, we are not returning to touch this earth." He opened his bag and took out two boxes of meals that we had prepared during our previous stop. We sat on the ground and finished our meals slowly. "Perhaps everything we heard was just stories, not reality," I said to my friend as we ate, "perhaps the valley was once like what we heard; now, it may not be occupied by any spirit or alien. Even if it is haunted or occupied by aliens, we might enter the valley, move freely, and return here under Lord Buddha's protection." "Without wishful thinking, no adventure can be undertaken," my friend retorted, "your wish is my wish as well."

We stood up and prepared to trek down the snow-covered slopes of the hill. We put on our snow boots, hooded our heads, grabbed snow sticks, and began our descent. It took nearly half an hour to reach the valley's plateau. We stood on the valley's rim and looked around. The valley's brightness and silence were oppressive. We began to make our way toward the valley's center. It was a slow walk, inching with trepidation at every step. We moved some distance, then stopped and looked back. The imprints of our footsteps on the white snow trailed behind us. They resembled stamps on the snow forming a signature of our last journey on this planet. We turned around and continued walking. We had only taken a few steps forward when we were abruptly separated as two identities divorced in space, whizzing and whirling up. I attempted to locate my friend. Half of his body was suspended in mid-air; the other half had vanished in a stupor. I discovered I was reduced to a pure concept as I concentrated on myself. My flesh had dissolved; my form had disappeared. I had only memories of the past. I was afloat in space. The invisible self within me had entered a different world.

I scripted a dot in space and, simultaneously, in my memory as I entered the new world. I wished I could come back here. I felt like I was being drifted by a current away from the dot the next moment. I couldn't see anything because I didn't have eyes. I couldn't hear anything because I didn't have ears. I couldn't smell anything because I didn't have a nose. I could not speak because I didn't have the organ of speech. I only had a mind to feel with and a self to experience. I was drifting away and away as if I only existed in infinite time and space.

I was moving slowly and then quickly, moving up and then down, feeling light and heavy. I was perplexed as to how I could experience all of this in the absence of sensory organs. "You are just an entity formed out of the intense and deep interaction of waves in the cosmic energy space," I heard from somewhere, "You experience because of the everlasting interactions and memories that you carry. Each interaction leaves a mark in your memory, creating the images you experience. If you didn't have a memory, you wouldn't have had any experience." It was a knowledge I had never known before.

I couldn't guess time because I didn't have an abstract reference in my memory to measure it. I had no idea how long I'd been moving like this; it could have been months or years. I was eager to meet the dot I'd left in the space. I was not sure when I'd arrive or if I'd ever see it again. I was afraid it would vanish or be removed from its original location. Then, my memory would be unable to locate it.

I tried to distance myself from my memory to avoid experiencing anything. The more I tried, the closer I got to it. My memory then began to play tricks on me. It started configuring strange images that I had never experienced before. It took me to different worlds where I came across shadowy living beings and living beings of other forms drawn on a sketchbook, as it were. I traveled through a series of long, dark tunnels. The darkness was deathly absolute. I was distressed, depressed, and panicked. I had a feeling I was doomed forever. But, at the end of the tunnel, I came across a vast expanse of bright light. I flew through it and experienced a transcendent bliss. I wished I could become one with it.

I faded with the games of my memory and tried again to break free from it. Finally, I could only become numb to the emotions it evoked in me. I was reduced to the status of a witness. No matter how strong my feelings were, they couldn't throw me off balance. My indifference taught me to experience only the self gradually. I learned to be calm and peaceful. I began to focus solely on my existence. The deeper I delved into my reality, the more I discovered it to be expansive. Gradually I realized it was ever-expanding and engulfing the entire space. Suddenly, I began expanding myself and was about to embrace infinity. I was afraid I would dissolve, and immediately I sprang back to attach myself to the memory again. But it was now a different kind of attachment with the memory, an attachment without factually being attached.

"Are these the realizations of Buddhist monks, or are there other kinds of realizations?" I wondered. I was unaware of the monk's meditation-assisted realizations. They undoubtedly elevated one to a higher plane of existence if they resembled these. They're also quite fascinating. At the same time, I wondered if these realizations were that significant in life. People could live their lives happily even if they didn't have them. There might be phases of grief and sorrow in life, which are just as fleeting as the phases of happiness. That's how life works. There might be exceptions where despair loomed large over a significant stage of one's life. Then, a sense of detachment would undoubtedly be supportive. However, there might also be other choices, such as instilling tolerance.

I was perplexed as to the significance of such realizations. I thought I had gone missing somewhere. The central idea could be something other than simply experiencing those realizations. The realizations could only be a series of events on the spiritual path to liberation.

I was curious if the aliens had a similar experience to me. Quite likely, I thought, they might not be thinking at all. They could simply live a life without any form. But could there be life

181

without intelligence? Could intelligence exist in the absence of thought? A slew of questions plagued me. "*If aliens could convert humans to their species, they must be intelligent. They should also have more advanced techniques than humans. That appeared to be quite mysterious. But, in an invisible world, everything is invisible,*" I reasoned, "*Perhaps the problem was the memory that I carried with me. Every mark on my memory formed a mental image of what humans would create. Aliens might have different types of memory, resulting in different imprints. At some point during my journey in space, I thought my memories would be gradually erased, and a new set of memories, similar to those of the aliens, would be created. I was terrified again because if it were true, I'd never be able to meet the dot I'd created in space.*"

In my mind, thoughts raced like horses. My memory created them. I had no clue how long I had spent like this. My mind gradually began to freeze. I was awake but on the verge of nodding off. The fear again gripped me that I would miss the dot I had created in space if I fell asleep. I became hyper-vigilant. I began to imagine the moment when I would meet him. I was ecstatic at the prospect of meeting him. What a joyous occasion it would be when we would meet together. This thought came naturally because I only had one friend in this infinite journey, the dot I created in space. I wished to be closer to him. The more I thought about him, the stronger my desire to meet him became. My journey continued in this manner.

While wandering in my world of thought, I suddenly experienced a bright expanse that was gradually transforming into a hallow. It began to entice me inside once it had fully developed. I blissfully traveled with it until we came across a great form in space. It was a divine form of Lord Buddha. When

I touched Him, the form vanished, and to my utter surprise, in its place was the dot that I had scripted in space. My joy had no bounds. I embraced it with unbridled delight. And at that very moment, the miracle did happen. I realized my feet had come into contact with the blanket of snow that covered the valley. I was surprised. I tried to feel my body. I could feel it, and I discovered I was dressed like before. I looked around to see if it was the same valley. As I turned back, I found my friend standing behind me. We rushed up to each other and hugged. We had never felt more joy than at that precise moment.

We walked up the valley's slope to its crest and took one last look at the valley from the top before beginning our journey back to the monastery. We stopped at the nearest halt for the night before continuing to the hilly tribes' settlement. When they saw us, they couldn't believe it. They said we met them three years later and kept asking if we had been to the valley. After we assured them of our visit, they took us to be monks in disguise. They were unwilling to accept that we were ordinary people like them. "You must be monks, or else you will not be able to return after visiting the valley," they said. "No, we are not monks yet, but soon we are going to be," we replied.

We left the settlement and reached the monastery in two days. The monastery had not changed in the least. We entered the sanctuary, looking for the two monks who became our friends. Finally, we could trace them. They were also surprised to see us after a lapse of three years and were initially skeptical that we had returned safely after visiting the valley. Then we described in detail our experience in the valley. They listened to us quietly and then said, "The senior monk is not well and has informed us that he will soon be leaving for the abode of Lord Buddha. If you want to meet him, you must do so at your earliest."

We met the senior monk the next day. He was sick, but his face still had a radiance to it. As we bowed down to him, he recognized us right away. "I am glad that you have safely returned from the valley by the grace of Lord Buddha, and also in good time," he said, "I'll be leaving this mortal body soon to spend eternity at the feet of the Lord." It was now our turn to talk to him. We sat in front of him and told him, "We could only return safely from the valley because of your blessings and express our willingness to be monks now that our mission has been completed. Please accept our willingness to enter into the monastic life." He gazed at our eyes for longer than it should have been and said, "Let it be so." We were ordained as monks. We made the monastery our home because we didn't have to return to our own homes.

Rat's Note

Robin entered the public rose garden and rushed down the narrow path that meandered through the bushes. He was as though in a hurry. All of a sudden, he heard a sweet voice call him from behind. Surprised, he looked around. There wasn't any. The same voice came floating up behind him as he took a step forward. Then he paused again, trying to figure out where the voice was coming from. And he guessed it came from a taller bush. Instantly he rushed to the bush and peered inside. There was no human occupation, nor was there any kind of animal whose voice could confuse him. He retraced his steps through the narrow path, but the story continued. That prompted him to dash from one bush to the next, eventually leading him to a bush near the exit gate. When he looked out the gate, he noticed his wife, Rummy, smiling at him.

"You, uh, uh, you?" he yelled.

"What's the harm in that? It's a public garden."

"You're right, but you were at home."

Rummy pointed out, "You were supposed to be on the market."

"I suppose I'm here for a reason," Robin explained.

Rummy replied, "Same here."

"Let's not fight a word war; instead, let's solve the problem."

"Well, If you must know," Rummy began, "I remembered a few more items to be purchased shortly after you left for the market. So I set out for the market. I discovered you hovering around the garden fences by reaching out. It caught me off guard; what were you doing there—a Middle Ages romance? I freaked out and walked silently past you into the garden."

"You're hilarious," Robin exclaimed, "but it'd be even funnier if you knew why I went to the garden." Her gaze was fixed on him.

"Well, you're familiar with the fish market," Robin explained, "and it's difficult to find fresh fish out there. I just happened to get one. I knelt over it to better look at it, then lifted its collar to see what was inside. It was close to the color of a tomato. I realized I'd have to haggle hard to get it at a fair price. I suddenly felt a lot of pressure inside the lower part of my bladder. That led me to the garden fences in search of a suitable place to relax. I went inside the garden to finish the task because there were so many people around. The rest of the story is already known to you."

Both of them burst out laughing. "Let me hook the fish while you finish your shopping and go home," Robin suggested.

Rummy went into the kitchen while Robin sat on the couch with the newspaper in his lap after returning from the market. It's routine for him to read every line of the newspaper, whether there's news or not. Rummy got him a cup of tea. "Two mighty warriors, Mohan Bagan, and the Muhammedan soccer teams will fight today at four p.m. in the Edens," he said without even looking at her.

"That's fantastic news for you; please arrive on time for the game," Rummy said.

"Don't worry; I'll be finished napping before the game begins."

He took a shower after finishing the news items. He was

radiant when he emerged. "What's the matter with you?" Rummy was curious, "You have an unusually bright appearance."

"Think about it: the film trailer in the garden, the fresh fish at the market, and the football game in the Edens all combined to create a romantic feeling that worked on me," Robin responded, "Take a shower, and let's finish lunch early."

Robin walked to his favorite spot in the house, the backside balcony. He was standing on the patio, with a small forest in front of him, and the surroundings were peaceful. He peered through the curly passage winding through the branches of the trees to catch a glimpse of the distant sky. At times, his mind flew away with the bird to an unknown destination.

He was startled to hear Rummy say, "Lunch is ready."

On the dining table was a plate of white steamed rice. On either side of the plate, there were two bowls. One dish featured potatoes in a poppy seed paste. The other had a large piece of fish half-hidden inside a thick mustard curry and half outside as if a small boat was half-submerged in muddy water. The plate's appearance poured out a lot of digestive juice into Robin's stomach. He did it all in one go. Rummy looked happy.

Nothing else to do; Robin went for his nap. "Wake me up before four p.m., if I don't," he said to Rummy before leaving. He awoke well before four p.m., tossed in his bed for a few minutes, and then got up to get ready for the match. He made himself at home on the sofa with two extra pillows, put on a loose dress, brushed his hair, and settled into a cozy spot. He switched on the television and navigated to the appropriate channel. Before the game began, a few advertisements appeared and then vanished on TV.

Like the race runners, team supporters have an idea of who will win. Robin's instincts told him that the game would end in a draw as the ball rolled out of the centerline and into the Muhammedan Sports Club penalty box.

When his son, Toto, hugged him from behind, he was watching the players' movements on the field with bated breath. Daddy and son were utterly engrossed in the soccer game. It was an indescribable pleasure for them to watch a game together.

"Look, Mohan Bagans is carrying the ball to the penalty corner and putting it on goal for a clean headshot," Robin said.

"Not so easy, it's difficult to breach the Muhammedan's defense," Toto said.

"I bet Mohan Bagans would win by one point."

"Not a bad day's dream!" exclaimed Toto.

"Did you enjoy your fish?" Robin inquired abruptly. "Fish, what do you mean?"

"Didn't you have some fish for lunch?"

"No, I had drumstick curry, lentils, and poppy seed potatoes," Toto explained.

"She might surprise you at dinner, but how did you get the drumstick?" Robin inquired.

"Didn't you get the drumsticks for lunch?" Toto asked.

"No, I had the mustard fish curry and the poppy seed potato."

"She might as well surprise you at dinner," Toto said before calling his mother.

Rummy showed up on the scene.

"What's the problem?" she inquired.

Toto responded, "Mom, Dad says he had fish for lunch."

"Where did the fish come from?" I peeled the drumsticks throughout the morning, cut them into pieces, and appropriately dressed them to make a curry before proceeding with the rest of the cooking. Your father was too preoccupied with the newspaper to remember anything."

"You're mistaken if you think you're going to bother me and take my attention away from the game. My attention is focused on each player, and my thoughts are on the football as it moves up and down," Robin explained.

"Same here," Toto replied, "But I guess you had something else going on before the match."

"What was it?" Robin inquired.

"You had a fish curry for lunch in your dream, which you ate while sleeping. The hallucinations are frequently so vivid that they lodge deep within the subconscious, erasing the immediate past."

"Don't be a jerk," Robin advised Toto, "inquire with your mother about what happened in the morning."

Rummy replied, "Nothing special."

"Didn't you perform a play in the garden?" Robin inquired.

"Why on earth am I going to do that?" Rummy replied.

"Don't pretend. After you finished your play, you went for shopping, and I went to the fish market. Back at home, I was reading the newspaper and learned about the match. That's how I'm sitting," Robin explained.

Toto was perplexed for a moment before saying, "I think I have the answer to the mystery. Dad had two dreams. In the first, he was in the garden, and in the second, he bought fish. He ate the fish for lunch during the second. The first erased reality from the mind, while the second erased truth."

"Enough with the nonsense you've spewed. How would I have known about the match if I had forgotten the truth?" Robin stated.

"It could have come in your dream," Toto replied.

"You mean, the truth was erased by a dream, and a portion of it reappeared in another dream? It's complete nonsense.

You've gone insane," Robin stated.

Rummy finally broke her silence. "Quite the contrary. You've gone insane; otherwise, how could you have come up with the bizarre idea of me performing a play in the garden?"

"I'm no lunatic to talk such nonsense, nor have I forgotten the immediate past, as Toto claims," Robin said.

"Look, I washed my black Tee Shirt before I took a shower and clipped it on the front balcony hanger," he said to Toto.

"If you go to the balcony, you will find skins of drumsticks that I pilled off in the gait," Rummy explained.

Toto dashed to the front balcony and returned a minute later, exclaiming, "Strange, the black Tee Shirt is hanging there. Mom, the skins of drumsticks are lying within the garbage pot as well."

"Let me now put an end to the matter," Robin implored.

He had a solemn expression on his face as if he was about to deal with a serious matter. "Compute factorial six for me and give me the correct value," he instructed Toto. Toto paused for a moment before responding, "Seven hundred and twenty."

"You're correct," Robin said. Is it that simple for a man to remember the answer if he has lost his mind?"

"Of course not," Toto replied, "but aren't they all so perplexing?"

Robin had no response. Rummy was quiet.

A rat appeared out of nowhere and vanished in no time. It left behind a note for the reader, not for Robin, Rummy, or even Toto:

"A modern story is no less abstract than modern poetry."

The Cabin Monk

"Everyone passes time on earth until he passes away," Deo said as he rolled on his bed. His wife responded, "Of course, he does, but for a reason. Whoever passes time without a purpose is called a useless person, and you are precisely that." For Deo, a new day had begun. He had seen it all before. Three mornings a week would begin in this manner. According to his wife, he had passed the point of redemption.

He could hardly do anything about it. He was like this from early on. He had never had any ambition in his life. He could do almost nothing except let things take their course. He had an ordinary education, an ordinary job, and an ordinary life. He had no feelings about marriage. His parents got him married. His wife offered him two children. He was happily playing with them. Then things began to fall into place. The children grew older, family demands increased, and the wife became frantic. He was finally labeled as useless.

He was never remorseful about it. He saw it as a natural progression of events. He knew that one day his grown children would look him in the eyes and silently convey the same message as their mother. He decided to leave the house on that day. He reasoned, "There's no harm in leaving the house once you are written off." He was silently waiting for that day.

Meanwhile, a fortune teller arrived at their home. His wife, among many other things, inquired about him, albeit reluctantly. The fortune teller gazed at him for a while, longer than it ought to have been, and said, "Although he appears useless now, he would be most useful one day." "When is that day?" the wife immediately inquired. "You'll have to wait," the fortune teller said. His life did not change as a result of the incident. His wife gave him the same look as she did before.

He narrated the story of the fortune teller to his friend, his only friend, who had stood by him since he was a child. He used to confide everything to his friend, who would patiently listen to his long stories and then calmly advise him on what needed to be done. He never went against his friend's advice. Upon hearing the story of the fortune teller, his friend said, "Who knows you might become a big man one day and would be the most desired person in your family. It all depends upon the chances in life whether you wish them or not." His friend didn't take even a moment to utter these words to him.

The same friend, when heard about his decision to leave the house, had much difficulty pronouncing a single word. For a long while, silence prevailed between the two. Finally, the friend broke the silence, "Leaving the house and family is not a decision which should be made impulsively even though many monks throughout history have done so. According to what I have heard, many psychic personalities also left the house impulsively. However, you are neither a monk nor a psychic. You are an ordinary person, just like me and thousands of other beings on this planet. So, you must exercise caution when making such a significant decision. And I, as your trusted friend, must carefully advise you on this matter."

He looked his friend in the eyes for a moment before saying, "Once you feel you've been written off by the family, you stay there as an object surrounded by a few living entities." If there is no interaction, it makes no difference whether the object is an animate or inanimate. The difference between the two is then the precious little. Even though I have no ambition in life, I don't want to live a life like that. I'd rather live alone, even if it's in the middle of a forest."

"There is a difference between living in a society and living in a forest," his friend responded and then continued, "humans, by nature, prefer to be surrounded by other humans, even if they do not interact with one another. The mere presence of others around you provides a sense of belonging, which is essential for human survival. You may wish to live a secluded life in the woods, but it is easier said than done." He decided not to pursue the subject any further after listening to his friend because neither his friend recommended nor rejected the idea of remaining in seclusion. He thought he might return to the subject at the appropriate moment.

The time breezed by. One day, his wife brought up a proposal to start a family business. She said that if the business becomes successful, then the entire family will be quite well-off. He listened to his wife's proposal and then responded, "I am not the kind who can do a business, nor do I have a strong desire to make money. I don't have any objection to you starting a business because you believe it will give you good money. You may go ahead with your two children." The wife said, "I knew you would not have any objection to us doing a business. But the real problem in starting a business is to get the initial capital. I could not save enough money that I can start the business." He remained silent for a while and then replied, "I too don't have any savings that I can offer you. However, I have some money accumulated in my service provident fund. If you want, I may give you that money to start the business. Although I may not join your business, I sincerely wish you to be well-off."

193

The wife quickly responded, "That's a great idea, and a nice gesture as well."

He drew the entire amount from his provident fund. That is something one would not normally do unless there was an extremely pressing need. His co-workers were taken aback and asked a series of questions. He didn't say anything. His silence sparked a flurry of speculation among his friends. He finally put an end to all speculations stating, "I wish to make a middle-age gift to my wife."

He handed over the money to his wife and said, "That's all I had. I suppose you could make a modest beginning with this amount and grow the business over time."

After many years, his wife smiled at him and said, "Thank you for the money. After all, you're not all that useless!"

The next day, Deo met his friend and told him everything. His friend looked into his eyes and said "So, you're preparing for your solitary life. Go ahead and let me know when you're ready."

"I told you about the day I am going to leave the house," Deo replied, "I'm looking forward to that day."

A few weeks later, Deo stood in front of his friend's door carrying a bag. His friend calmly opened the door, asked him to take a seat, and began, "Finally, the journey begins. But where do you wish to go? Have made any concrete plans? If not, tell me if I can help you."

Deo answered, "You have stood by me since I was a child and advised me on what to do in all difficult situations. Although I do not consider this to be a difficult situation because it is my creation, I would like to seek your help and advice."

His friend stared at Deo and asked, "Are you serious about leaving the house and leading a secluded life?" Deo quickly answered, "Of course. That is why I have come." His friend began, "You must have seen those mountains, some distance away from our place. Some of those mountains belonged to my grandfather. He was a wealthy man in his neighborhood with a lot of property. He passed away forty years ago. My brother and I inherited the mountain portion of his fortune because no other relatives were interested. We had no intention of profiting from this fantastic property that we owned. It was just a property in our name. We didn't need the mountains, and the mountains didn't need us. My brother's only contribution was the construction of a cabin near the mountains. I was young at the time and assisted him in making the cabin. Occasionally, he used to live in the cabin for a few days and then returned home. Later, when I grew up I used to visit the place. It was an interesting experience for me. There was nobody around me. There was no one to talk to. I could read a lot, and think things over. At the night, I could hear the cacophony of animal sounds coming from the woods. Hearing those sounds, I used gradually fall asleep. In the morning, amidst another chorus of dissimilar sounds, I used to get up. I enjoyed a different life there." His friend paused, took a deep breath, stared him in the face, and asked, "Do you want to live there? It is not in the middle of the forest, as you desired, but certainly on the edge of it."

Deo said softly to his friend, "It appears to be a place that I was looking for. But I'd like to hear your thoughts on my staying there, as I've always followed your advice on my problems." His friend remained silent for a few moments before saying, "You could try out there for a few months. I've never stayed out there for an extended period. So, I can't tell you how you'd feel if you stayed there for the rest of your life. If you adjust in a few months, I believe you will be able to stay there permanently. If you don't, we'll work out some alternatives." "Stay with me for today," his friend continued, "We'll visit the place tomorrow."

At five thirty a.m., Deo and his friend went to the car park, where they boarded a green sports car. "Because it's a long drive, we'll stop for lunch along the way. If we get hungry in the meantime, I have a few packets of assorted snacks in my backpack. We'll consume them," his friend said. Both drove through city streets that appeared to be sleeping in the early morning hours and finally made it onto the highway after a while of driving. The car was running at speed of 90 mph. There were a lot of pickups in the specially tuned car. His friend effortlessly was changing gears and shifting from one lane to the other smoothly in between other cars. Deo told his friend, "Driving is a risky enough sport." His friend with his hands on the steering wheel turned toward him and said, "Don't worry. I am not going to have an accident. I am a careful driver. I keep my car in tip-top condition too."

His friend turned on the music. It was some fast-track music. The tunes were familiar to Deo. He asked his friend, "Do you like this kind of fast track music?" His friend replied, "Music fills in the silence. Fast track music stimulates your consciousness and keeps you alert. If I listen to Beethoven's music, an utterly perfect piece while driving, I might want to close my eyes and die right then and there only. That does not mean I don't adore Beethoven. At dusk when the sky is feathered with a few brush strokes of white clouds, I might turn on Beethoven, close my eyes and sublimate to my surroundings. Don't you like fast-track music?" Deo responded, "I do. But I never knew that it helps driving as I never owned a car."

While his friend glanced at the watch and went back to humming along with the music, Deo was looking on either side of the road. Green lands spread out like carpets on either side.

196

Rows of trees ran parallel to the road at times blocking the view of the green lands that stretched far away. The billboards on the road relayed their messages to none. After about half an hour of driving this way, his friend said, "We shall be stopping at a good restaurant within fifteen minutes of drive and have our lunch."

His friend pulled into a rest-stop restaurant for lunch. Deo ordered fish curry and rice and his friend ordered roasted chicken and salad. He enjoyed the food very much and asked for his friend's opinion. His friend replied, "This is the best restaurant on this highway. Whenever I come on this side, take lunch or dinner here. I am glad that you enjoyed the food as well." They climbed back into the car. The car accelerated on the highway. His friend turned on the music and began humming along. After a while, his friend looked at Deo and said, "The place we're going is deep in the mountains, not the most pleasant dwelling in the world. You will not be able to see anyone else while you are there. There is also no communication channel. You'll be on your own. Solitude manifests itself in various ways. It will be of a certain type, which may surprise you. Be ready for that." Deo nodded quietly.

His friend exited the highway and began driving down a smaller road. A small town was located on a side road near the exit. His friend stopped at a small shop and purchased a large number of groceries as well as packets of instant food. Deo reached for his wallet, but his friend shook his head and paid it all off. They got back into their car and drove down the road. With one hand on the steering wheel, his friend said, "All these groceries will help you survive there for a month." After that, I'll pay you another visit and stock your kitchen. This will continue until you decide to return. If you don't, it will last until either you or I say goodbye to this world."

Once they left the little town, nothing was visible except the road in front and the occasional car that passed by. The road was so narrow that two cars could hardly pass each other. As they drove along, a sharp bluff on the left appeared out of nowhere. It looked as though there was a mountain stream down below. Thereafter, curves on the road got sharper, the road more slippery, and the rear of the car spun a couple of times. Deo opened the window. A rush of cold air entered the car. They were making their way up the hills and deeper into the mountains. As they weaved through the sparse forest, they heard the magical sound of the trees. They continued driving through the sparse forest until his friend slammed on the brake and the car came to a halt. A house, a log cabin, stood in the foreground.

Deo opened the door of the car and stepped outside. High above him, the wind rustled symbolically. Patches of chill hung in the air. He zipped up his jacket. His friend coming out of the car slowly approached the cabin and walked up the porch steps. Deo trailed him. "Welcome to my house," said his friend. Deo entered the house. The cabin was made up of a single big room. There was a small bed in the corner, a dining table, two wooden chairs, and a worn-out sofa. A large lamp hung from the ceiling. There was also an old chest for storing cloth. The kitchen was simple with a work surface. There was a small gas stove, a big gas cylinder, a sink, and a pail. A pan and a kettle were on the shelf, as well as a frying pan hung from the wall. The toilet was located next to the kitchen. There was also a black wood-burning stove in the middle of the large room.

Deo looked out the window. Within a short distance, the dense forest was visible. The mountain range hides beneath the sky, edging the forest. A small stream ran nearby. He could hear the faint sound of water from a short distance away. His friend filled the kettle with mineral water, placed it on the stove, and turned on the gas. Then, drawing Deo's attention, his friend said, "You need to clean up the house a little bit. It would take you a day or two to complete. Make your bed as comfortable as possible. On the top of the chest, there are a few bed covers and two blankets. They are suitable for their intended use. In the toilet, there are two buckets. You have to store water in the kitchen, toilet, and in buckets as you need them. You could hear the sound of water in the stream as you were watching out the window. The stream runs down the mountain and a channel of water flows within a quarter mile of here. You might drink it and bring it here in buckets." Deo took a look around and stated, "It appears to be a good place to live. The majority of the necessities for daily living can be found here. I don't think I'll need anything else than what you've provided in the cabin." His friend poured hot water from the kettle into two cups and dipped it in two chamomile tea bags. While drinking the tea, he took one last look around the cabin and said, "Before I leave, let me give you a few more information. Firstly, the gas could run out in about a month. Don't worry, I'll bring a new gas cylinder on my next visit. Second, don't venture too far into the woods. It's extremely dense, and there's no way to get through it. In case you go inside the forest, keep the cabin in sight. It is easy to get lost if you go farther, and it is difficult finding your way back. I experienced it once. Finally, remember you are out of any communication system. In an emergency, I wouldn't come down off the mountains. You are cut off from the rest of the world. In my next visit, I shall find out how was your experience of living a solitary life was. See you then." Giving his last set of sermons, he got down the stairs and entered the car. The car rolled slowly down the narrow path.

Once his friend was gone, Deo plunked down on the chair. There was an abrupt void. He felt lonely. He felt lonely among his family members many times, but that was a different kind of loneliness. This loneliness was an experience he had never known. He sat on the chair for a long while looking perhaps at nothing. Then he got up and walked over to the window. The sky was blue with light white clouds sweeping across the mountain tops. The wind rustled through the branches of the tree. The faint sound of spring water filled his ears. His loneliness slowly began to fade. Suddenly, the mountain, the sky, the clouds, the forest, and the unseen spring gave him a sense of belonging. This was again an experience he never had before. He stood in front of the window for quite some time until the pale Lavender dusk began to spread over the mountain peaks. From the window, he could see the birds flying in a full circle before diving into the forest. He could feel the onset of the evening and could imagine that a lacquer blackness would soon cover everything as one blanket. He turned around and approached the large lamp suspended from the ceiling. He ignited it. The room began to glow. He felt a lot better. He walked over to the kettle and added some more water to it. By the time the water began to boil, he surveyed the kitchen shelves and planned how he would arrange the groceries on top of them. After finishing his tea, he began organizing the kitchen with all of the items his friend had purchased for him.

After finishing the work in the kitchen, he felt tired and hungry. He took out a packet of instant food and put it on the stove to cook. He devoured the entire food in no time. Then took a bottle of mineral water, drank half of it, washed his hands, and splashed himself on his face. It was already dark outside. He walked over to the bed and properly arranged it. He felt sleepy all of a sudden. It had been an exhausting day. He turned off the light and plopped down on the bed. He shut his eyes. His mind was slowly going blank. The last thing he remembered was thinking about how he was going to spend his first night in the cabin. He was fast asleep in no time. He didn't even wake up once before morning.

When he got up, a beam of morning sun landed on his face. He lazily watched a white cloud move from one edge of the window to the other. He stood up from his bed and looked around. The room seemed to be bigger than what he saw yesterday. He walked over to the kitchen and looked at the rows of mineral water bottles. He picked up one of them and thought, "This is the last bottle I should be using. The remainder would be kept on hand in case of emergency. The first thing that he has to do this morning is to fetch water from the stream." He poured half bottle of water into the kettle and with the rest; he washed his face and quenched his thirst. He put the kettle on the stove and turned on the gas. Once the water had boiled, he poured it into a large cup, dipped a tea bag in it, took out a muffin, and sat calmly in a chair near the dining table. He ate his breakfast slowly, looking out the window. Then he stood up, took two buckets from the toilet, a towel, and a shot from his backpack, and then exited the cabin. He followed the sound of water and arrived at the stream in a matter of minutes.

The stream was narrow. One could cross it easily. The dense forest started from the other side of the stream. He sat on the grass near the stream and gazed around. On one side, he could view the mountains. The stream was flowing from that side and running down for a short distance before disappearing into the forest. The dense forest's tall trees cast a green veil over the sky in the foreground. He looked up. Patches of light clouds drifted slowly across the sky. He sat there quietly for a long time, listening to the sound of the water flowing.

He filled buckets with water and bathed in the stream. He had never had such a refreshing bath before, and he immediately decided that the first thing he would do every morning would be to go to the stream, fill in the buckets, and immerse himself in water for as long as he wanted. He returned to the cabin slowly, holding two buckets in his hands. He filled the pail with water, put some in the pan, and filled two empty bottles. He put a full bucket of water in the toilet. He was pleased with the arrangement for his daily water requirement.

Nothing else to do he sat on the chair and looked around. He discovered a self in the corner of the room packed with worn-out books. He remembered his friend telling him that during his occasional visits, he used to spend time here reading books and doing a lot of thinking. He got out of his chair, walked over to the bookshelf, and looked at them. All kinds of books were stacked there, from history to modern philosophy. On top of the shelf, several storybooks and novels were specially arranged. He picked up a storybook and began flipping through the pages. They were a little sloppy, but he could read through the pages. He planned to relax after lunch by reading one of those books. He went into the kitchen, looked around, and took something to cook for his lunch.

He finished his lunch and lay down on the bed, picking up a book from the book himself. As he turned the pages, his eyes gradually closed and he fell asleep. It was evening when he awoke. As he looked through the window, he could see the sun in the sky placed just over the mountain peak. He did not know the time as he didn't have a watch. He only knew that in about half an hour, the sun would set behind the mountain and the dusk would spread all over the place. He sat on the bed for a while before getting up to make himself some tea. The dusk had already settled in as he sipped his tea. He could hear the birds humming outside as they returned home.

After finishing his tea, he rose from his chair and turned on the lamp. He picked up the book from the bed and began flipping through the pages. It was a collection of ghost stories. The ghost of the first story could do anything as long as the master kept it engaged. Unengaged, the ghost would enchant the master and make him do whatever it pleased. So, while the master was napping, he instructed it to climb up and down a bamboo until the next order.

He finished the first story and looked outside. It was already dark. He went to the kitchen, stood there for a while to plan the menu for the dinner, and then took the items from the shelves of the kitchen. He started preparing his dinner. After dinner, he took the storybook again and read a few more stories. Finally, he retired to his bed. He had extinguished the lamp. The room was pitch black. Through the window, he could only see the sky. A few stars peeped through a tear in the cloud. From outside, the sound of rustling leaves came floating in his ear. He tried to sleep by closing his eyes. However, the mind wandered over a variety of objects. He allowed his mind to wander; at times he was merely a spectator, at others, he was deeply involved with the object. He didn't care about the hours of the night and didn't know how long his mind floated like this. Suddenly, he heard a mixed chorus of animal sounds. It went on for a long time. Hearing those sounds, he dozed off, just like his friend did when he used to visit this place.

He awoke later than usual in the morning. For him, a new day had begun. He lazed around on the bed because he knew he wouldn't have to deal with any new task of the day. It would be just like the day before. He could, at best, bring a change by spending more time near the spring. Only in this manner did the days pass by. Initially, it was all a new experience for him. But, as the days moved ahead, he reckoned a droning sense underlying everything. After that, he passed days by crossing out dates on the calendar. He had some strange experiences as well. On some nights, he would wake up suddenly. For no particular reason, he felt the urge to walk through the room, from the bed to the kitchen only to discover that silence alone rolled like oil all over. On some days, sitting on the chair, he used to feel as if he alone was at a standstill, the rest of the world kept on moving. He hadn't any idea about when his friend would pay him another visit, but he was desperate to see him.

Suddenly, one day he saw the green sports car standing in front of the cabin. He dashed down the stairs and hugged his friend. They both lifted every item from the car and placed it in the cabin. He poured some water into the kettle and turned on the gas. His friend looked around the room, kitchen, and toilet before he took his seat on the chair. "You have organized everything in the cabin so well that I am amazed. However, you don't appear to be so poised," he said. Deo brought two cups of tea, handed over one to his friend, and took a seat on the other chair. After settling down, he replied, "You are correct and then he narrated every bit of his experience over the last month." His friend stared at his face coolly all the while he was narrating his experiences.

After he finished, his friend said, "I had some inkling about what you said because I stayed here before, but not for a long time. I could envision the consequences of staying here for an extended period. As I previously said, solitude manifests itself in one form or another, and you must deal with it in the beginning. But, do you want to go back?" "I am in a quandary," he replied, and then continued, "I'll be shifting from a new kind of loneliness to an old one. That's all there is to it. I had previously considered it several times. I was at a loss for words. I was desperate for your guidance. Tell me what the best option for me is now that you're here." For a while, silence hung between them. Then his friend began, "You have three choices. First, you are free to return home. However, it would be somewhat embarrassing for you and your family. Second, you may decide to change the location, which both of us can agree on. Finally, you may conduct another month-long trial. Who knows, maybe you'll gradually adjust to the situation." There was another pause between the two. Finally, Deo said, "Tell me what you would have done in this situation." "I would give me another chance," was the quick response.

His friend had left him in the same predicament in which he was spending his days. Through the window, he could see his friend's green sports car slowly rolling down the road. Nothing new could his friend offer to him. He sat down on the chair to think about what he should do. But he knew that whatever he decided would not be implemented before his friend's next visit. That made him realize he had a large window of time to think about things, and he felt relieved. He got up from his chair to make another cup of tea for himself and began to plan his dinner. After finishing the meal, he took a book from the shelf and attempted to flip through the pages. But he was unable to concentrate. Their mind wandered through random thoughts that he had never imagined. It was a sort of self-discovery. He had no idea that his inner mind was so clouded with uncertainties. He had always considered himself to be an ordinary man, with modest ambition and little drive. So he had nothing much to lose. Why, then, did his mind become unsettled by his solitude? He should've just shrugged it off. But the mind was playing a different game. He stayed in that state of mind for a long time and then, he gradually fell asleep.

The following day went off as before. He lingered a little longer near the spring. His bond with the spring grew stronger as the days passed. He began to spend the entire midday lying down on the grass near the spring. He passed the time by gazing at the sky, perhaps looking at nothing, or staring at the façade of the dense green forest on the other side of the spring. He was gradually drawn into remaining in a state of emptiness. His inner restlessness waned, and he gradually gained the confidence to face the challenges of loneliness that had arisen in his life.

On the next visit, his friend looked him in the eyes and said, "Perhaps on my next visit, I shall find you fully prepared to spend your life here." He replied, "The solitude that engulfed me is no longer as hard on me. But I'm still not at ease with it." They shared tea and talked about a variety of topics. Before leaving, his friend mentioned a few books in the shelf that he might find useful in passing the time in his current state of mind.

He had almost created a routine for his life. The days mostly went by without incident. But, memories played tricks on him at times. He used to become engrossed in his past life, reminiscing about his family and incidents that had never bothered him. He used to feel helpless. He didn't know how to come out of those memories. He reasoned that the thoughts were meaningless to him at the present state of affairs and made an effort to shake them off his mind. But, they would come back with vengeance and wreck him. The only choice that was left to him was to put up with them till they faded away on their own. He took refuge in it; it paid him off. Gradually in this way, he learned to distance himself from memory. He went past all that happened before and stopped looking back. He never looked into the future as he didn't have one. He learned to live for a single day.

His friend was overjoyed to see him at the next meeting and commented, "Now you'll be able to spend the rest of your life here." I didn't expect you to reach this point in such a short period. I have to admire your tenacity. As I promised before, I have to only stock your kitchen once a month until both of us live on this planet and don't have to worry about you on anything else." He responded, "I could make a home here because of you alone, and could also sustain myself here because of you alone. I have to admire you instead of you admiring me."

Time flew by. The days turned into months. Months became years. He made the cabin his permanent home and lived a fairly routine life. His inner self was only changing. He became quieter day by day and formed a stronger bond with the spring. He grew fond of listening to the sound of water lapping at the spring's edge. He'd close his eyes and get lost in the melody of the sound as if he were listening to Beethoven. He was gradually drawn into it to the point where he forgot the time. He fell asleep at times while listening to the sound of water. That was only the beginning of a much greater transformation. The sound of water converged within him to create a unique sound with a blend of divinity that was difficult to describe. He used to be immersed in it for a long while, and on occasion, he would fall into a trance, neither sleeping nor waking. He used to feel an indescribable inner joy when he came out of it.

He would return to his cabin and finish his routine work after spending his favorite hours near the spring. Then he'd sit on the chair, holding a book in his hand. He steadily became interested in philosophical books over time. He'd read a few pages of the book and start pondering over things he'd never thought about before. The thoughts eventually converged on the priceless question of life's meaning and purpose. This way of thinking continued for a long time until one day he discovered that the cognition of every object in the surroundings is itself false, only a fantasy. He questioned himself about the reality of the very existence of the universe. He didn't find a concrete answer, but he did realize that everything is a mental construct. When one stops thinking about something, it is no longer there. His experiences with spring music informed him of this. He gradually leaned toward emptying his mind and becoming aware of himself. He would frequently sit on a chair on the small balcony, gazing out at the forest. The surroundings would be completely silent. Even the sounds of the wind used to be swallowed up by the grand expanse of the forest. In that silence, his eyes would gradually close; his mind would gently let go of all thoughts, and he would slip into deeper silence. He relished remaining in that state for as long as his mind would allow.

There was another change in him, admiration for nature in its purest form. In autumn, he would discover everything in the forest had taken on a desolate cast, the colors swiftly fading before his eyes. During the rains, he would enjoy the greenery flowing down from the hill. In some inconspicuous night sky, he would stare at thick cloud cover breaking, and from within, a lovely half-moon would illuminate the façades of the forest. On another night, he would experience the silence of the night being split by the cry of a bird, and then, once the bird was out of sight, the silence flowed back in, as if a viscous fluid filling in every opening. On some nights, he would close his eyes while sitting on the balcony chair. On his retina, the particles of darkness would form mysterious patterns. Patterns that degenerate without making a sound, only to be replaced by new patterns. As he opened his eyes, darkness, but only darkness would shift like

208

mercury in motionless space. He learned to read nature's messages written in all things; in leaves of the forest, in the rocks, in the clouds, in the flowing water.

His friend noticed the changes in him over time. During one of his visits, his friend stared at his face for a long while before making a few remarks that surprised him. He said, "Your hairs are as white as mine; your long beards look black and white; you have a few faint lines on your forehead, and your eyes gleam with a soft glow. You look more like a monk." He replied, "I don't have a mirror to see my face. It has been years since I have seen my face. Of course, I could feel that I have grown hair and a beard too. But, I didn't have any idea about what color they had chosen to display. Thanks for reading my face. As for the eyes, you might have seen your own eyes in mine. Finally, it makes little difference to me whether I look like a worn-out man or a monk." "It makes a difference to me," his friend said, adding "I can now proudly announce that I know a monk who also happens to be my friend." He replied, "It is all your creation. You made me a monk if I am a monk at all today. I have nothing to say if declaring me a monk makes you happy. I have always accepted what you have told me. But what difference would it make?" Prompt was the reply, "Wait for a few days."

After a few days, his friend returned accompanied by a group of people with him. "These people want to meet you, talk to you, and seek your advice on how to live a sane life," said his friend as they all entered the cabin. He calmly looked at his friend and replied, "I wonder if I could give them any useful advice. They all appear to be content and knowledgeable. I'd be delighted to discuss any topic of their choice with them. Because my knowledge is limited' I'm hoping to learn rather than offer them new information through the discussions." The talks went around

209

any number of topics, from day-to-day concerns to highly philosophical ones. Everyone was energized, delighted, and captivated by his deliberations. Before leaving, they sought his blessing. His friend was staring at his face the entire time he spoke, as well as keenly observing the reactions of others. "I had to start somewhere," his friend said after everyone had left. I knew you'd handle the rest. He replied, "Why do you want all these? I came here to live a quiet life. You helped me to fulfil it. But, why do you want to take it away from me now?" Then, he became quite. His friend allowed a few moments of silence to prevail between them and began, "You have achieved much more than what you wanted. Now it is your turn to give. To solace others is an act of humanity. You are first a human being, then a monk. And, having walked on a razor's edge, you are acutely aware of the mind's game and despondency. I hope and believe you will serve people for their benefit." "I have never said anything against you and have always followed your advice. But my mind tells me it won't end where you expect it to," he said.

On and off, people would come to see him. At first, he was able to handle them nicely. However, as time passed, the number of visitors increased, and he found it difficult to manage them. His friend came to his aid and suggested that he appear in front of the window for a limited time, offer his wisdom, share his experiences with nature, and finally, bless everyone who came to meet him. This was a practice followed for a long time. But, after a few years, it became impossible to keep up. Visitors had turned into devotees by that point, and they were only interested in his blessings. Then, his friend suggested that he sit in a high chair near the window and put down one of his legs through it. To receive his blessings, the devotees would approach him one by one and place their hands on his feet. He used to sit like that twice a day, once in the morning and once in the afternoon. To manage the devotees, his friend built a nice fence around the cabin and a gate for entry.

Suddenly, one day he saw a hue and cry near the gate. A lady, accompanied by two young people, attempted to push through the gate, defying the Que. He noticed his friend appear out of nowhere, spoke with the people in the Que, and finally let them in through the gate. His friend escorted them to the cabin. After a little while, he heard a female voice say, "I could never imagine you would be such an important person. People are waiting in line to visit you. It's simply incredible. I had to inform the people at the gate that I was your wife. They weren't prepared to believe it. We would not have been able to come to you as easily if your friend had not been present." When he turned around, he saw his wife, who had grown old like him, standing there with her two sons. He greeted them and asked them to wait until he had completed his task of appeasing the devotees.

He climbed down from his chair after the morning session and inquired about their well-being. He also asked how their business was doing. To that, his wife said, "The real business is about to begin. We may abandon our current business to devote our full attention to the new venture." His friend cut in and told him how his wife discovered everything and how she made her way up to this point. He listened quietly to his friend and said, "As I said before, things aren't going to end where you expect them to. They would go far beyond the holy task of serving others. Because you have always come forward to solve my problems; you may have to solve a larger problem that I see in front of me."

It was his wife's turn to speak, and she had a lot to say. She began, "After you left us, we had to work extremely hard to establish the family business. Our efforts were largely successful, and we were doing well. We grew accustomed to our way of life over time. We didn't miss you as such, but we missed your presence on certain occasions. I learned about you from your devotees and then met your friend, who was candid enough to tell me everything that had happened. Now, I have a proposal for you as you are a sought-after individual and I happen to be your wife. I've already spoken with your friend about it. He neither opposed nor enthusiastically accepted my proposal. He left it up to you to decide."

He fixed his gaze on her and said, "I can guess your proposal. You want to make a profit from the services I offer. To be frank, I did not volunteer to serve the people. It was my friend's suggestion. I acted the way he wanted me to because I had always listened to him. The result is what you see today. I came here to live a peaceful life, which I earned the hard way and, of course, with the invaluable assistance of my friend. My peace was initially disturbed by this type of service, but I gradually distanced myself from the service that I presumably provide. I can now do it with detachment. If I accept your proposal, I'm not sure I'll be able to keep my distance."

His wife responded, "I am well aware of your noble goal and your loyalty to your friend. In my opinion, your friend suggested the most appropriate action for you to take. If you want to live a saintly life, service to others must be a part of it. That is exactly what you are doing. That makes me extremely happy and proud. There are two ways to look at what I'm about to propose. The first is, of course, how you perceive it. The second approach would be to think of it as volunteering for the benefit of your family members. You're not acting in your interest. Remember what the fortune teller said: ' You'd be the family's most useful member one day'. You could be a saint while also being useful to your family. Nothing is wrong with it. We would ensure that you remain the saint as you were."

He retorted, "The fortune teller also said you had to wait. I am sorry that you had to wait so long to find me useful. Anyway, tell me what's on your mind so that I can decide what's best. Of course, I'll consult with my friend before making any decisions." His wife responded, "The devotees are known for their generosity toward their master. They want to spread their master's name and message to every nook and corner. At the same time, they wish to make the master's place memorable. They are generous in their contributions for this reason. What I propose is very simple. I'd like to establish trust in your name. The trust's sole goal would be to look after the devotees' well-being and to perform charitable deeds. You don't have to utter even a single word to your followers about this. You continue to do exactly what you are doing, and we promise not to interfere with your peaceful life."

He turned to his friend and said, "As I said before, you have to solve a bigger problem for me. It is right in front of you. I shall abide by your solution."

His friend replied, "I would have been happy if you had made your own decision. But I knew you wouldn't do that and would instead leave it to me. To be honest, I don't see any difficulty in your wife's proposal as long as your wish and your wife's one remain mutually exclusive. I have an apprehension, only an apprehension, about whether reality will allow the two wishes to be together. It necessitates a high level of discipline. If both of you can keep it up in the early stages of your journey, the problem will be solved elegantly. Promises are only made to be broken."

"You are here to observe us," his wife said to his friend. I believe in you just as much as your friend does. If you notice that your friend is being bothered in any way, I will leave my task and return. I'm used to living a tumultuous existence."

His friend quickly responded, "Once you start, you can't stop. Devotees would be harmed, and nothing could be worse. Furthermore, once you arrive, you will be able to look after my friend. My presence would be no longer required."

He reacted immediately to what his friend said. "You cannot break your promise. You would stock my kitchen once a month until both of us leave this planet. Then, only, I can live an independent life and venture to live my life in the manner in which I was living. You can't abandon me."

His wife appeared content and reassured.

Within a year, the surroundings of the log cabin had undergone a momentous transformation. The cabin's surroundings were peppered with cottages, rest stops, waiting rooms, and eating establishments. Devotees had access to all facilities while visiting the cabin monk. They were all content, and their contentment increased the trust's wealth and convenience.

Deo used to live his life in the cabin as he had before. His family members only peered into the cabin on rare occasions to see their most useful and important member of the family.

The cabin monk was well-known in and around the small town of Trichi. Devotees did an outstanding job. They promoted their master to the rank of a well-known monk in the area. They'd also given their master a new moniker: "Deo-Baba."

Until today, trainloads of devotees arrive in Trichi to touch the feet of "Deo-Baba." Some devotees believe he lived for one hundred and fifty years, while others believe he lived for two hundred and fifty. Nobody knows for certain how long he lived. People, who could have told how long he lived, have passed away. The Log cabin has been well maintained by the trust, which is run by the generations of Deo. A wooden leg hangs down the cabin's window. At what point of time, the human leg was replaced by the wooden leg had faded into the distant past. Those who beheld the human leg being replaced by the wooden leg are no longer present. Devotees can now witness the wooden leg swinging slowly in the breeze on a quiet autumn evening. Inside the cabin, the soul of the "Deo-Baba" rests in peace, listening to the melody of the spring.

The Trio

"I am drifting nowhere, like you," she said after a brief pause. They got along reasonably well at first. They thought they had a lasting relationship, but it soon fell apart. A silly word implying something shook everything, and it never recovered. They'd been walking down a long, dark alley, as it were, in peace. In some ways, her departure was caused by circumstances beyond his control. What was done was done, and so on. It didn't matter how they got along over the last few years.

"Why do things happen the way they do?" Jimmie pondered. He grew up in a typical town and attended a typical school. He went to college at eighteen, had an ordinary first romance with a girl, and graduated with an ordinary degree. After graduating college, he and one of his friends established a standard printing service. It did not last long. They diversified into various occupations. Everything was so mundane! As if it were an ordinary stream flowing ordinarily over an ordinary terrain. It could have flown like that until it became entangled in a large river or vanished into the aridity of a desert. But it didn't. It came across a boulder large enough to deflect its course on a bed of pebbles, which caused ripples in its path now and then, eventually leading it to wander in the vast expanse of unevenness. He had never intended to be a drifter, but the strange course of events beyond his control led him to this situation. Perhaps his life would have taken a different path if he hadn't met Ilina! His wife would not have requested a divorce if she was not afraid of being drifted away to nowhere.

Jimmie met Ilina in Joe's bar, holding a glass of beer. She was a reporter. "This is Ilina, who visits my bar on the most irregular of schedules," Joe said. Then he turned to Illina and said, "This is Jimmie, my best friend who pays me irregular visits." "What an unusual introduction!" Jimmie said as he stroked his friend's hand. They met in the bar more frequently after the first meeting. They'd traded books, talked for hours, and filled the ashtray with cigarette butts. About her background, he knew very little. He learned her father was a professor through their endless talks on different matters. Her mother was a floor dancer. An ever so curious match one could think of.

From Joe's bar, their meeting place steadily shifted to pubs and the nearby university campus. On some weekdays, she would drop into his apartment, cook together, fill his ashtrays, and dance to rock music. The following morning, they would walk through the woods of the university campus, have lunch in the dining hall, and have a cup of coffee in the student lounge. They would stretch out on the grass and gaze at the sky if the weather were good.

He remembered an eerie afternoon. They were out for a walk, hands in their pockets. The yellow leaves brought down by winds turned the footpaths into dry beds of gold. As they walked, not a sound to be heard except for the crunch of the leaves under their feet and the piercing cries of the bird. Suddenly she blurted out, "Why are you silent today?" "Just like that," he said. They kept walking a bit before sitting down by the side of the footpath. She took a drag on her cigarette. "You don't want to talk about what you are brooding about, do you?" "Not today; I feel like keeping silent." She flicked her half-smoked cigarette to the dirt and began drawing abstract patterns on the ground with a twig.

"Do you schedule your days? "Like?" she asked, frowning at him. "The things you intend to do tomorrow." "I don't have a tomorrow or a yesterday; I only live for today," she replied. "A new day would begin at the end of the night, anyway; you could call it whatever you wanted," said Jimmie.

She said, "Rather, a new set of events would begin; only events move, while time remains frozen." Even the earth's rotation around the sun is merely an event that creates day and night. For me, every day is today."

"Of course, it's a matter of interpretation." But don't you want to plan the events?" "Differences between two interpretations amount to very little."

She tossed the twig to the ground, stood up, brushed the dry bits of grass from her coat, and then continued, "We may like to stroll aimlessly over the continent of the arbitrary as some rootless winged seed blown by the breeze."

He asked, "Where do we go now?" "Back to the apartment," she said. They thrust their hands back into their coat pockets and slowly returned to his apartment.

Throughout the year, they often met in the nightclub or on campus. In one of those night sittings, Jimmie shifted the conversation to his friend—Jack. She was resting on the sofa, half laid with a pack of cigarettes on her side and listening to him. As he narrated how Jack left home with a Buddhist monk, she suddenly sprang up, sat upright on the sofa, and gazed at him, transfixed. She yelled, "Why don't you tell me everything you know about Jack?"

Jimmie said, "I didn't know much about Jack's background except that he came from a rich family. With no siblings, he was the family's sole offspring and would use his position to disagree with his parents on almost every issue." Jack's father was a lawyer who tried to steer him in that direction. But he flatly refused, claiming he had no interest in law. Then his father suggested he study engineering. He, too, declined. After a brief pause, his father asked him which path he preferred. He quickly responded, "Philosophy." "Very well," his father said.

Jack attended university to pursue a degree in Philosophy. During his studies, he used to argue with his father over seemingly minor issues. Arguments could last for hours. The father would speak like a lawyer, while the son would talk like a philosopher. One focused on facts, discoveries, proofs, and interrogations. The other roamed the realms of interpretations, illusions, myths, prejudices, and natural laws. But, beneath it all, both appreciated the clarity of expressions, rhetoric, and orations. "At best, I might acknowledge the cognition and the cognitive world that you talk about," the father said in one such bizarre argument. The rest of your premises are hazy and elusive." "Cognition is nothing but fantasy," the son replied, "only an accepted meaning is asserted on it. The commonly accepted definition is utilitarian. It is never possible to explain true cognition by arranging and rearranging words. The explanation would only demonstrate the verbal correlation between utility and cognition. Thus, the negation of cognition corresponds to the negation of utility and language. And without utility and language, existence ceases for the individual, and everything devolves into chaos. So, to avoid chaos, one must acknowledge cognition, which is why you acknowledge it. But, simultaneously, you must acknowledge the fantasy that you consider vague and unclear."

Father stared at him awhile and said, "I think you would have done better in carpentry."

Finally, Jack received his Philosophy degree and accepted a

voluntary job with a charitable organization. Most evenings, Jack and I used to meet at our friend Joe's bar to discuss whatever we wanted over beer cans. Joe's first bar was located in the basement of a building. It was a small bar with only a few sittings.

It was a warm summer evening. The city was bathed in pale lavender dusk. A strong breeze blew between the buildings above the ground. The bar in the basement was full. I was assisting Joe with customer management. Jack walked into the bar late at night after most customers had left. "Any important office engagements?" Joe inquired. "No, I was just speaking with a Buddhist monk who is visiting the organization," Jack explained, "An interesting person to have a conversation with; having an innocent look and a glow on his face; he can talk on varied topics with amazing fluency. He appears to be well-versed in both western and eastern philosophies. We had a lengthy conversation, but it went extremely well. Perhaps I spoke with someone so calmly for an hour for the first time."

Slowly, Jack stopped visiting the bar. Joe and I wondered what had happened to him. The two might have developed a special relationship, a spiritual communion. Though spiritual communion was not a recognized course of study in Philosophy, Jack was very inclined toward it. That was why he took up a voluntary job in a philanthropic organization.

After about a month's absence, Jack reappeared in the bar. "Hope you still enjoy it," I said as I handed him a can of beer. "We thought you left town with the monk deserting all of us," I continued. After a few sips of beer, Jack replied, "Perhaps I'll do that. That is why I have come here. I figured I'd better tell you about it. I'm quite taken with the monk. Even if I rearrange my words, I won't be able to express how I feel about him. Before becoming a monk, he was a regular researcher who studied eastern religious philosophy. It allowed him to study Buddhism, and he became so enthralled that he left everything to become a Buddhist monk."

I intervened, "I have no idea about Buddhism. Nor do I want you to enlighten me about it. I have one question: why do you want to go with him, leaving everything behind?"

"In search of that which exists beyond the cognitive world," Jack responded. He continued, "I haven't read much about Buddhism, but my discussions with him piqued my interest. Throughout my studies, I maintained that cognition is a fantasy, a myth, and that the universe is a product of our minds. I often wondered if there was any truth behind the level of cognition. The monk has a similar viewpoint and is looking for the truth."

"Did you talk to your father?" Joe inquired. "Not yet," he replied.

Joe continued, "I wonder if you would ever become a monk, but both of you have similar pursuits. You may wander with him to any part of the world searching for what you wish to search for, but I am afraid you can match his way of life. You are brought up in a different environment, and adopting a different way of life is not easy. Finally, I wish to ask you if seclusion is obligatory for searching for the truth."

"You're probably right," Jack replied, "I'd never become a monk, but I'd like to wander with one in search of what I'm looking for. I am fascinated by the idea of looking beyond the cognitive world, and the fascination can only take one of two paths: it can blossom into overwhelming love, or it can perish. If my fascination wanes, I might return and have another sip of beer in your bar. Changing one's way of life is a secondary issue; after all, the monk was a regular research fellow before becoming a monk."

"I only have one favor to ask you," Jack continued, "I'd appreciate it if you could meet the monk once."

"Of course," Joe said.

Three of us went to see the monk the next day. He sat in a chair and looked out the window. As we entered the room, he turned around with a smile. Joe and I both looked at him, taken aback. It took some convincing for us to believe that a man's face could be as innocent as a child's. "Jack told me a lot about you," he said as he greeted us and continued, "You are bonded and look out for each other as close friends. Caring is a natural beauty that unites us all. Even when we aren't aware of it, we care for one another and form the most enthralling illusory universe." "We are ignorant of the subject of philosophy, unlike you and Jack," Joe and I retorted, "we trade in the most material world while pretending to be philosophers at odd times. Our philosophy consists of a few evasive words that begin and end on the verbal level. We deduced from Jack that you share our friend's philosophical viewpoint and that both of you would be leaving town soon to trade the unknowns."

"You are correct; ours share the same goal," the monk responded, "but if you claim to be ignorant of philosophy, I'm afraid you are mistaken. Humans are philosophers by nature, and their collective wisdom formed the subject of philosophy. Who knows, maybe your evasive language is pursuing the same goal as your friend but in a different way." The discussion lasted a long time and covered a wide range of topics. Finally, the monk expressed his best wishes to Joe and me and waved his hand goodbye.

Following the meeting, Joe and I told Jack, "Go ahead if you've decided to leave town with the monk." But please stay in touch."

Jack had a similar conversation with his father as that he had with us. His father stared at him without comments. Then he said, "If you have decided, I hardly have anything to say. Any moment you feel like coming back, welcome back home."

On an inconspicuous morning, Jack left the town with the monk.

Jimmie ended the story with his friend. Ilina crushed the butt of her last cigarette in the ashtray. Outside, night birds kept up a low cooing. A startling white moon shone in the middle of the sky.

Jimmie met her a few days later after that historic night sitting. They ate lunch in the university canteen and walked through its woods. There was complete silence. They looked up as they were walking. Occasionally, gaps in the blanket of green leaves would allow a glimpse of the blue sky.

"Aren't we getting too used to each other?" Ilina asked, breaking the silence.

Jimmie looked her in the eyes to see if she had any edge in her voice, but the words came out of a serious face. "We are used to living on this earth, but never spell it out," he replied. "We don't want to discuss it."

They walked together for a while with their hands in their pockets before sitting down on the edge of the path. Ilina lit a cigarette, took a long drag, and began, "Sorry for breaking the silence. Just pay attention to what I'm about to say. You are not required to speak if you do not wish to. My question was directed as much at you as it was at me, and your response was evasive. Trust me, this question had been bothering me for a few days, and even though it had nothing to do with it, I felt lonely for no apparent reason. Indeed, there must have been some reasons for me to feel that way, but they remained incomprehensible.

Probably, I am a drifter, and if it is true, then that might be the reason for me to be in the state I am."

"Since the silence has been broken, let me speak whatever I feel like," Jimmie said, "First and foremost, I apologize for making you feel that way. It was undoubtedly not on purpose. Second, you must have one of three temperaments to be a drifter: religious temperament, artistic temperament, or psychic temperament. You can't be a drifter if you only have one. If you have two coexisting, you will be a drifter for the rest of your life."

"Which ones do you believe I have?" she inquired, looking him in the eyes.

"You know them better than I do; if you ask me, I can guess two for you—the temperaments that cause you to dance passionately and see every day as today," he responded.

"Which is to say I'm a drifter?"

"I'll leave you to figure it out."

"You mean I have a psychic temperament?" she asked, tossing a half-smoked cigarette on the ground before standing up and brushing the dust from her coat.

"Having a psychic temperament is not wrong; religious temperament is also a type of psychic temperament." They began to walk back to his apartment.

Ilina arrived at Jimmie's apartment after a week. They cooked together, danced to rock music, stuffed the ashtray with cigarette butts, talked about various topics, and then retired late at night. Jimmie awoke late in the morning, raised a cigarette to his lips, took a long drag, and searched for Ilina. There was complete silence everywhere. He climbed out of bed and searched the entire apartment. He was the only one there. He didn't expect her to leave without saying anything to him. Suddenly, he noticed a folded paper slipped beneath the ashtray.

He lifted the ashtray, took out the paper, and opened it. It was a note from Ilina. She wrote, "I am leaving the town for what I do not know. A force, an inside force, is driving me to leave the place, and it is beyond my control. I wonder if I will ever meet you again. But I still love you."

He plunked down in the chair with the paper in his hand and gazed absently at it. Time passed by. His heart ached. He felt withered away. A piercing bird call shot through the window, a call he had never heard before that resounded in his heart. He sobbed. He had never cried so much before.

She had been gone for a month. Nothing changed from day to day except loneliness, which sucked him in inch by inch. He led a meaningless routine life. He got up at seven o'clock, ate breakfast, went to work, ate dinner out, had a few drinks, came home, climbed into bed, and turned off the light. That is how it went. He went through the days in the same way that people cross out days on a calendar. One quiet evening, he suddenly remembered he hadn't been to Joe's bar in a long time. He took out his jacket and got started.

"So, how is everything going? It seems like a long time since I last saw you, "Joe stated as he approached.

"Not that well," Jimmie replied.

"You appear to be different."

Jimmie sat near the counter, opened a can of beer, and drank half of it in one sitting. Joe inquired, "How is Ilina doing? I haven't seen her in a long time."

Jimmie looked at Joe without saying anything. "She had left town," he said, pulling her note from his pocket and handing it to him.

Joe took a look at the note. He then read it a few times before speaking up.

"Why didn't you share it with me?"

"I was trying to face it alone, see myself in the mirror, and try to put my strength to the test."

"What was the outcome?"

"A hollow inside me that never filled up, as if waiting to be sucked into some whirlpool of fate."

Jimmie drank another can of beer and then narrated the entire episode to Joe. There was silence between the two.

"Somethings are forgotten, vanish, and die," Joe said, breaking the silence. "However, this was hardly a tragedy in the grand scheme of things. I'm not sure what to call it. A passing drifter wave most likely hit you. The wave had passed, but the pulses lingered; the song had ended, but the melody persisted, and so on. "I'm afraid those pulses will become lodged in your void over time."

Jimmie looked him in the eyes, amazed. Joe was known to him as a practical man who was cheerful with clients and amusing with friends. However, this Joe was one-of-a-kind, with a philosophical tone and prophetic wisdom. Joe hit the correct node in him, awakening him to the fear that was haunting him. Loneliness was slowly devouring him, but it was also slowly changing him. He took a minute to think before speaking. "According to the monk, humans are philosophical by nature. Your words could not have better supported his claim. It takes me by surprise."

Joe started with a faint smile, "Bar has been my teacher since the beginning. It taught me the business and how to feel people, make them happy, smile in despair, and listen to what should not be listened to. It increased my instincts more than anything else. As I served my customers, my instincts would follow me around the bar."

"What do those instincts do?"

"They would collect stories of human hopes and despairs, sorrows and joys, successes, and failures, loves and betrayals. I trust my instincts as I move from table to table around the bar. The stories are meaningful to me up close, but as I move away, they gradually become a jumble of sounds and finally a noise as I reach behind the counter. From afar, the intense human emotions appear to evaporate into the alcoholic fog. My teacher taught me that distance is important because the massive stars appear to twinkle in the sky from a solar distance. I am concerned about the distance you have with the episode. I'm sure it's still within you. Body cells replace themselves every month, even right now," he continued, "most of what you know about something is made up of memories. And all of these memories fade into distant memories that are difficult to recall. You will be sucked into your fear if you cannot distance yourself. You'd be a nomad for the rest of your life."

Jimmie had been in awe of Joe the entire time. After briefly pausing, he said, "I wish Bar were my teacher. However, wishing is not the same as doing. He drank one more can of beer, hugged him, and bid him farewell."

Jimmie showed up at Joe's bar a week later. Joe motioned with his hand toward a stool in front of the counter. He sat on the chair, rested his hands on the counter, and waited a few moments before asking, "How proficient are your instincts in hearing silent words?"

Joe smiled at him, offered him a can of beer, and said, "You're leaving town; the journey of a drifter begins."

"Right, you are. There is no telling even what will happen a month from now. But, the only certain event is my leaving the town. I wonder if it would help me in any way, but I am driven by force, as it were, to this destiny. I imagine a winged seed blown away by the unforeseen breeze."

Joe replied, "You are well aware of a drifter's virtue. Probably, it might open up a new avenue for you to search for the same great truth as our friend is looking for; remember what the monk said."

Jimmie left the town, traveled to many places, and took up any job. Most often, it had been at a gasoline station. Otherwise, at a drink bar; at a bookstore; or on a radio station. He never got hooked on any work for a long while. He would save some money through the job and then eat through his savings. Once the savings were over, he would take up another appointment. Initially, he did not know whether he was cut out for this life. He feared he might open the wrong door someday but could not back out. But gradually, he got used to it.

He met the girl he married while working one of these odd jobs. In the beginning, they were friends. He had no idea why she had chosen him to marry. When he asked about it, she replied succinctly, "There is something about you." He decided not to delve any further. What would he say if something was discovered in him? Everything went seemingly well at first. They believed they had reached a long-term agreement. But it crumbled sooner or later. She was probably singularly methodical, had an utterly realistic grasp on her life, and desired a home—the opposite of what he turned out to be. She was terrified of swaying. In retrospect, that was the best guess he could make about her. She once inquired, "Had you wanted children?" "No, can't say I ever wanted kids."

Before the divorce, she said, "Maybe if we'd had a kid, it wouldn't have come to this; what do you think?"

"There are lots of couples with kids who get divorced."

Probably, he never should have gotten married, at least never to her.

Jimmie moved around like the desert wind. He went along with the flow of events. Yesterday, today, and tomorrow all merged into one for him. Nothing got into him, and he didn't get stuck to anything. Everything around him flowed and floated. He would have moments when he felt his mind was empty, with distorted images drifting and diffusing.

The time flew by. One fine morning, he awoke with a strong desire to return to his hometown. "How long has it been since he left town?" he pondered. He couldn't recall anything specific. He got on a long-distance train with no luggage. Exhilaration washed over him; no pending work, no complicated human involvement, no one wanting him, and no one wanting something from him. It was his hometown, but it was no longer his hometown. The train continued, and the sky turned a rainy grey, beneath which stretched the same monotonous scenery.

When he arrived in his hometown, he went straight to Joe's bar.

"What's the point of staying in a hotel?" "You have a home, don't you?" Joe inquired. "Why not just stay there?"

"It's no longer my home."

Joe remained silent on the subject.

Joe's bar had changed drastically. It was no longer that dark basement. It was out onto the hillside and was on the third floor of a building complex. It had large windows that faced west and north. The colorful hills could be seen through the bar's large windows.

Jimmie was drinking a beer. The latest hit music was being played through the ceiling speakers. Joe kept his gaze fixed on him the entire time.

"So, everything is different now."

"Got married and divorced; you know how things go between two people. I shouldn't have gotten married."

"What about you?"

"I have forgotten what married life is like. It's been so long. She died years ago."

Joe set to making some fancy cocktail and a salad for a customer, and while doing that, he pulled out an envelope from the drawer. It was a reasonably big size envelope. He handed it to Jimmie. Jimmie frowned at him and then opened it. A neatly drawn pencil sketch came from within—a man trying to hug the sky, stretching out his hands in vain to embrace it.

"That's a mail received from Jack."

"*Hmm*, the search is still on. Any idea where could he be?"

Joe replied, "For sure, not hanging between the heavens and earth."

"What do your instincts say about his attaining the goal?"

"Maybe, he is nearing the truth; he wanted to know."

"What makes you say that?"

"The sketch."

Jimmie remained silent for a while before taking a few sips of beer and speaking up, "Truth does not exist in the heavens or on Earth. It's within you. Of the inevitable flow of events, we are drifting away from the truth. If only we could put a stop to it! The only hope is that 'everything returns'. If we follow the flow, it may return us to the point from which we were taken."

Joe replied, "Probably, you are right. But the truth can be realized in many ways. Our friend may be following a path to sublime himself to go beyond the realm of cognition. He always thought that the truth, if there is any, is beyond the level of cognition."

Jimmie said, "Your teacher, it seems, taught you also to put things always in a nice way. What else did you learn from him after I left?"

"Not much. Only the cocktail of sounds that formed the noise stopped bothering me anymore. The noise filtered through the ears for sure, but the brain refused to process it. Probably, it got boring doing that. From behind the counter, I could sometimes see the actions of dumb human patches diffused over a blanket of smoked cigarettes. At other times, I gazed absently at the human figures, silence separating me from them. I felt as if I was an observer, purely an observer."

Joe's bar was starting to fill up around seven o'clock. Jimmie was about to leave when he said good night to Joe. "Come tomorrow if you have time," Joe said. "Sure, if I stay for tomorrow," Jimmie replied.

Jimmie emerged from the bar. One of his favorite roads was along the river. He moved toward the river to rejoin the road. He began to walk through it at the same rate as the river. The river was breathing to him. It was still alive. "The town belonged to the river from the beginning, and it would always be that way," he told himself. The new leaves on the trees planted along the banks were fragrant. There was a lot of green everywhere. He began walking along the coastline. Bewilderingly enough, the old jetty was still there. Now a jetty without an ocean was an odd creature indeed. He stretched out on the jetty and looked up at the sky. The sky was full of clouds, and it was starting to rain. He rushed back to the riverside road, and by the time he could get a taxi, a rain platter had fallen heavily. To the hotel, he said to the driver.

"Here on a trip?" asked the driver.

"Yes."

The following day, Jimmie left the town.

After a ten-year gap, Ilina came to the town driven by an impulse. She walked through the university campus and passed by the small coffee shop where she used to hang out with her friends. It had changed a lot; what hadn't changed was the list of coffees, the clientele, and the hard rock. She entered the woods near the university campus. She walked slowly down the path, her mind cluttered with distant memories. Suddenly, she felt Jimmie's presence. He was walking by her side, hands in his pockets. There was complete silence. They continued walking for a short distance before sitting down by the side of the path. She looked up from there to glimpse the sky through the patches of green leaves. A twig landed on her head unexpectedly. She lifted it from her head and felt it; it was a real twig. She awoke from her trance and found herself alone on the path, surrounded by greenwood trees. A nearby bird was cooing softly.

She emerged from the woods and made her way to the town center. On the way, she passed by the apartment she had visited so frequently. She paused in front of it for a moment. It appeared—how should she put it? "A painfully solitary structure." She continued on her way to Joe's bar. It wasn't in the same spot it used to be. She looked for it and eventually found it in a place she could never have imagined. It was in one of the hillside's posh areas. She took the elevator to the third floor of a multi-story building. She noticed a nicely carved wooden board hanging on the wall with the writing, "Joe's Bar." She entered the bar.

It was around six o'clock at night. There weren't a lot of people inside. She walked right up to the counter, sat on the high stool in front of it, and ordered a can of beer. A young man in his twenties served her. She sipped her beer and then inquired,

232

"Where is Joe?" The man looked at her as if reading something and replied, "He no longer lives in town."

"Can you tell me where I can find him?"

"Well, he left town two years ago; didn't say where he was going," the man continued, "but before he left, he asked me to look after the bar and, if necessary, he would be in touch with me; I am his son." "As I approached the counter, I could guess it. You have your father's appearance. Your father and I have known each other for a long time. I used to frequent this bar when it was located in the basement."

"You have to be Ilina. "I hadn't seen you before, but I'd heard a lot about you from my father," he continued, "and two of his other close friends are there." He displayed one of the hall's walls.

Ilina took a look at the wall. It was a large wall with a large window on one side. Colored hilltops shone through it in the last rays of the sun. The rest of the wall was taken up by three large paintings framed side by side. She got up from the stool, walked slowly toward the wall, and stood there in front of the paintings. They were clear and shining in the lamp's light, and would attract the attention of any visitor. She gazed at the pictures intently. The first was a man in space, attempting to hug the blue sky with his hands stretched in vain to embrace it, "Jack." The second one was a winged seed blown about on the random wind, "Jimmie." And the third one was a large bottle of beer covered on top with hat-wearing blue specs looking out the bar from the counter, "Joe."

The time breezed by coldly, solidly, and rigidly; how long she did not know. When she turned back, she found the young man standing behind her with a can of beer in his hand. She took it from his hand and said, "Thanks," and continued, "love flows like the wind, carrying all of us together and hugging every bit of the creation. Yet, looking at us from a distance, it stands aloof, serene, and divine." The man looked at her with awe and said, "I shall remember these words. If I ever get in touch with my father, I shall convey your words to him about the paintings." Ilina said, "Thank you for everything. Keep smiling. Goodbye." She walked out of the bar slowly.